The Princess and Curdie

GEORGE MACDONALD

Chariot Books
Elgin, Ill.—Weston, Ont.
Scripture Union
London

*Other books by George MacDonald
in this series:*

The Princess and the Goblin
The Lost Princess
The Golden Key and Other Stories

First printing, November 1978
Second printing, April 1979

First published in book form 1882
First published in this edition 1978
by Chariot Books—ISBN 0-89191-165-0
and Scripture Union—ISBN 0 85421 657 X
Printed in U.S.A.

Contents

About George MacDonald

As his name suggests, George MacDonald is Scottish, born in the rural town of Huntly, Aberdeenshire, in 1824. He lived to see our century open, dying in 1905.

It was a humble beginning for the author of about twenty novels, several theological and similar works, six full-length fantasies for which he is most remembered, a number of delightful short fairy stories, and much poetry. But the Scot never lost sight of his humble life as a child and young person, and we catch many glimpses of the countryside he knew and loved in his stories.

He was devoted to his father, from whom he learned the meaning of God's fatherhood. His father was the head of a small weaving business, who owned some fields. The family lived in a little house called Bleach Field Cottage, so-called because the fields around were used for bleaching. His mother died when George was eight, and his father married again; the boys got on well with the kindly step-mother. The cottage was so small that George slept in the attic. He was happy boy, riding, climbing, swimming, and fishing, and also lying reading on the back of his favourite horse. George greatly loved animals and natural things. His now forgotten novels hark back to this rural world, and helped to inspire a Scottish movement in literature called 'The Kaleyard School'.

Being very clever (later in his life he was, like C. S. Lewis and J. R. R. Tolkein in our time, scholar as well as storyteller) George went to Aberdeen University in 1840, working in the long vacations to pay his way. Here he began his writing career. For a few years he struggled as a tutor to some rather unpleasant children in London, but his life was brightened by meeting his future wife, Louisa. He received a call into the Congregational Church, and entered Highbury Theological College in North London. His first church was in Arundel, where he fell into disfavour with the deacons, who reduced his small salary to persuade him to leave. Some of the poorest members, however, rallied around with offerings they could ill afford. Then he moved to Manchester for some years, preaching to a small congregation and giving lectures. The small family (there was now one child) were always on the brink of poverty. Fortunately, the poet Byron's widow, re-cognising George's gifts as a writer, started to look after the family financially. They moved down to London, living in a house then called 'The Retreat', near the Thames at Hammer-smith, later lived in by the famous poet and storyteller William Morris. It was a large house which had lots of room the rapidly growing family.

Many famous writers and artists came to visit the MacDonalds, as well as people who shared a social concern for London's desperate poor. One famous friend was 'Lewis Carroll', who let George read an early version of *Alice in Wonderland* to his children. They loved it, and the author enlarged and published it. One of George's sons, Greville (who later was to write his father's biography) remembered calling a cab for the poet Tennyson.

George MacDonald became Professor of Literature at Bedford College, London, and once read his fairy story, *The Light Princess,* to his students instead of giving a lecture. A person who lived at the same time (Ian Maclaren) described him as 'the most Christlike man of letters of his day'. In 1878 'The Retreat' was sold, and thereafter much of George's life was spent in Italy, largely for health reasons.

The writer C. S. Lewis learned more than anyone else from George MacDonald. Lewis said that what he did best was the making of myths, that is stories that can't easily be forgotten, stories that seem of great importance and full of meaning. Usually, myths are not made by individuals, but he felt that MacDonald was the greatest individual myth-maker of which he knew. The most important meaning of MacDonald's myths or marvellous stories is holiness, which nearly always conveys joy. Such stories often shock us 'more fully awake than we are for most of our lives'. Lewis believed that his greatest myths were to be found in his adult books *Phantastes* (1858) and *Lilith* (1895), as well as in the children's stories *The Princess and the Goblin, The Princess and Curdie, The Lost Princess,* and *The Golden Key* (all of which are included in our series). He says that in these 'the meaning, the suggestion, the radiance, is incarnate in the whole story'.

C.D.

The Princess and Curdie

Introduction

Some readers think that *The Princess and Curdie* is the greatest of George MacDonald's books. It is a sequel to *The Princess and the Goblin* but can be read without having read the first book.

Curdie deliberately kills a white pigeon and then feels deeply sorry. He begins to realize what the pigeon *is*, and thus what all creatures really *mean*. He had only known the pigeon as a fact, without any meaning. Curdie places his hands in the ancient Queen Irene's burning roses, and receives the magical and wonderful gift of being able to tell people's real nature, or meaning, by touching their hands.

The Queen allows him an ugly, misshapen animal called Lina to help him in his adventures. Holding its paw, he discovers the soft hand of a child. The child is the real nature, the nature towards which it is growing. As a contrast, many of the humans that Curdie meets have beasts inside them. As in so much of life, things are not what they seem.

One wonderful feature of the story is its power of make-believe, or invention. The string of misshapen creatures which appear out of the forest and follow Lina are vivid and real. But MacDonald's make-believe is most clearly shown in the convincing world that he makes up in this story. This can be seen especially in the city of Gwyntystorm, which has a distinct medieval flavour, and in the varied country regions that lie between it and the ancient Queen's castle.

This story has a sort of happy ending, like all proper fairy stories. The princess and Curdie marry, and their kingdom is peaceful and happy. At the very end of the book we are told, however, that the city of Gwyntystorm, temporarily uplifted by their goodness, falls into wickedness again after their deaths. It is finally destroyed (as are so many civilisations) as a fitting punishment. The story ends in Biblical prophecy, on a sombre but real note.

But there are many joyful and hopeful notes to the story. Not least is the disguised ancient Queen at the feast. This idea of disguise is common in many kinds of stories. In the greatest story of all, God is dressed as a humble man. The Queen's service at the feast strangely and beautifully echoes that of Christ at the Last Supper.

Colin Duriez

1978

CHAPTER ONE

The Mountain

CURDIE was the son of Peter the miner. He lived with his father and mother in a cottage built on a mountain, and he worked with his father inside the mountain.

A mountain is a strange and awful thing. In old times, without knowing so much of their strangeness and awfulness as we do, people were yet more afraid of mountains. But then somehow they had not come to see how beautiful they are as well as awful, and they hated them — and what people hate they must fear. Now that we have learned to look at them with admiration, perhaps we do not feel quite awe enough of them. To me they are beautiful terrors.

I will try to tell you what they are. They are portions of the heart of the earth that have escaped from the dungeon down below, and rushed up and out. For the heart of the earth is a great wallowing mass, not of blood, as in the hearts of men and animals, but of glowing hot, melted metals and stones. And as our hearts keep us alive, so that great lump of heat keeps the earth alive: it is a huge power of buried sunlight — that is what it is.

Now think: out of that cauldron, where all the bubbles would be as big as the Alps if it could get room for its boiling, certain bubbles have bubbled out and escaped – up and away, and there they stand in the cool, cold sky – mountains. Think of the change, and you will no more wonder that there should be something awful about the very look of a mountain: from the darkness – for where the light has nothing to shine upon, it is much the same as darkness – from the heat, from the endless tumult of boiling unrest – up, with a sudden heavenward shoot, into the wind, and the cold, and the starshine, and a cloak of snow that lies like ermine above the blue-green mail of the glaciers; and the great sun, their grandfather, up there in the sky; and their little old cold aunt, the moon, that comes wandering about the house at night; and everlasting stillness, except for the wind that turns the rocks and caverns into a roaring organ for the young archangels that are studying how to let out the pent-up praises of their hearts, and the molten music of the streams rushing ever from the bosoms of the glaciers freshborn.

Think, too, of the change in their own substance – no longer molten and soft, heaving and glowing, but hard and shining and cold. Think of the creatures scampering over and burrowing in it, and the birds building their nests upon it, and the trees growing out of its sides, like hair to clothe it, and the lovely grass in the valleys, and the gracious flowers even at the very edge of its armour of ice, like the rich embroidery of the garment below, and the rivers galloping down the valleys in a tumult of white and green! And along with all these, think of the terrible precipices down which the traveller may fall or be lost, the frightful gulfs of blue air cracked in the glaciers, and the dark profound lakes, covered like little artic oceans with floating lumps of ice.

All this outside the mountain! But the inside, who shall tell what lies there? Caverns of awfullest solitude, their walls miles thick, sparkling with ores of gold or silver, copper or iron, tin or mercury, studded perhaps with precious stones — perhaps a brook, with eyeless fish in it, running, running ceaselessly, cold and babbling, through banks crusted with carbuncles and golden topazes, or over a gravel of which some of the stones are rubies and emeralds, perhaps diamonds and sapphires — who can tell? — and whoever can't tell is free to think — all waiting to flash, waiting for millions of ages — ever since the earth flew off from the sun, a great blot of fire, and began to cool.

Then there are caverns full of water, numbingly cold, fiercely hot — hotter than any boiling water. From some of these the water cannot get out, and from others it runs in channels as the blood in the body: little veins bring it down from the ice above into the great caverns of the mountain's heart, whence the arteries let it out again, gushing in pipes and clefts and ducts of all shapes and kinds, through and through its bulk, until it springs newborn to the light, and rushes down the mountainside in torrents, and down the valleys in rivers — down, down, rejoicing, to the mighty lungs of the world, that is the sea, where it is tossed in storms and cyclones, heaved up in billows, twisted in waterspouts, dashed to mist upon rocks, beaten by millions of tails, and breathed by millions of gills, whence at last, melted into vapour by the sun, it is lifted up pure into the air, and borne by the servant winds back to the mountaintops and the snow, the solid ice, and the molten stream.

Well, when the heart of the earth has thus come rushing up among her children, bringing with it gifts of all that she possesses, then straightaway into it rush her children to see

13

what they can find there. With pickaxe and spade and crowbar, with boring chisel and blasting powder, they force their way back: is it to search for what toys they may have left in their long-forgotten nurseries? Hence the mountains that lift their heads into the clear air, and are dotted over with the dwellings of men, are tunnelled and bored in the darkness of their bosoms by the dwellers in the houses which they hold up to the sun and air.

Curdie and his father were of these: their business was to bring to light hidden things; they sought silver in the rock and found it, and carried it out. Of the many other precious things in their mountain they knew little or nothing. Silver ore was what they were sent to find, and in darkness and danger they found it. But oh, how sweet was the air on the mountain face when they came out at sunset to go home to wife and mother! They did breathe deep then!

The mines belonged to the king of the country, and the miners were his servants, working under his overseers and officers. He was a real king — that is, one who ruled for the good of his people and not to please himself, and he wanted the silver not to buy rich things for himself, but to help him to govern the country, and pay the armies that defended it from certain troublesome neighbours, and the judges whom he set to portion out righteousness among the people, that so they might learn it themselves, and come to do without judges at all. Nothing that could be got from the heart of the earth could have been put to better purposes than the silver the king's miners got for him. There were people in the country who, when it came into their hands, degraded it by locking it up in a chest, and then it grew diseased and was called *mammon,* and bred all sorts of quarrels; but when first it left the king's hands it never made any but friends, and the air of the world kept it clean.

About a year before this story began, a series of very remarkable events had just ended. I will narrate as much of them as will serve to show the tops of the roots of my tree.

Upon the mountain, on one of its many claws, stood a grand old house, half farmhouse, half castle, belonging to the king; and there his only child, the Princess Irene, had been brought up till she was nearly nine years old, and would doubtless have continued much longer, but for the strange events to which I have referred.

At that time the hollow places of the mountain were inhabited by creatures called goblins, who for various reasons and in various ways made themselves troublesome to all, but to the little princess dangerous. Mainly by the watchful devotion and energy of Curdie, however, their designs had been utterly defeated, and made to recoil upon themselves to their own destruction, so that now there were very few of them left alive, and the miners did not believe there was a single goblin remaining in the whole inside of the mountain.

The king had been so pleased with the boy—then approaching thirteen years of age—that when he carried away his daughter he asked him to accompany them; but he was still better pleased with him when he found that he preferred staying with his father and mother. He was a right good king and knew that the love of a boy who would not leave his father and mother to be made a great man was worth ten thousand offers to die for his sake, and would prove so when the right time came. As for his father and mother, they would have given him up without a grumble, for they were just as good as the king, and he and they understood each other perfectly; but in this

15

matter, not seeing that he could do anything for the king which one of his numerous attendants could not do as well, Curdie felt that it was for him to decide. So the king took a kind farewell of them all and rode away, with his daughter on his horse before him.

A gloom fell upon the mountain and the miners when she was gone, and Curdie did not whistle for a whole week. As for his verses, there was no occasion to make any now. He had made them only to drive away the goblins, and they were all gone — a good riddance — only the princess was gone too! He would rather have had things as they were, except for the princess's sake. But whoever is diligent will soon be cheerful, and though the miners missed the household of the castle, they yet managed to get on without them.

Peter and his wife, however, were troubled with the fancy that they had stood in the way of their boy's good fortune. It would have been such a fine thing for him and them, too, they thought, if he had ridden with the good king's train. How beautiful he looked, they said, when he rode the king's own horse through the river that the goblins had sent out of the hill! He might soon have been a captain, they did believe! The good, kind people did not reflect that the road to the next duty is the only straight one, or that, for their fancied good, we should never wish our children or friends to do what we would not do ourselves if we were in their position. We must accept righteous sacrifices as well as make them.

CHAPTER TWO

The White Pigeon

WHEN in the winter they had had their supper and sat about the fire, or when in the summer they lay on the border of the rock-margined stream that ran through their little meadow close by the door of their cottage, issuing from the far-up whiteness often folded in clouds, Curdie's mother would not seldom lead the conversation to one peculiar personage said and believed to have been much concerned in the late issue of events.

That personage was the great-great-grandmother of the princess, of whom the princess had often talked, but whom neither Curdie nor his mother had ever seen. Curdie could indeed remember, although already it looked more like a dream than he could account for if it had really taken place, how the princess had once led him up many stairs to what she called a beautiful room in the top of the tower, where she went through all the — what should he call it? — the behaviour of presenting him to her grandmother, talking now to her and now to him, while all the time he saw nothing but a bare garret, a heap of musty straw, a sunbeam, and a withered apple. Lady, he would have declared before the king himself, young or old, there was none, except the princess herself, who was certainly vexed that he could not see what she at least believed she saw.

As for his mother, she had once seen, long before Curdie was born, a certain mysterious light of the same description as one Irene spoke of, calling it her grandmother's moon; and Curdie himself had seen this same light, shining from above the castle, just as the king and princess were taking their leave. Since that time neither had seen or heard anything that could be supposed connected with her. Strangely enough, however, nobody had seen her go away. If she was such an old lady, she could hardly be supposed to have set out alone and on foot when all the house was asleep. Still, away she must have gone, for, of course, if she was so powerful, she would always be about the princess to take care of her.

But as Curdie grew older, he doubted more and more whether Irene had not been talking of some dream she had taken for reality: he had heard it said that children could not always distinguish betwixt dreams and actual events. At the same time there was his mother's testimony: what was he to do with that? His mother, through whom he had learned everything, could hardly be imagined by her own dutiful son to have mistaken a dream for a fact of the waking world.

So he rather shrank from thinking about it, and the less he thought about it, the less he was inclined to believe it when he did think about it, and therefore, of course, the less inclined to talk about it to his father and mother; for although his father was one of those men who for one word they say think twenty thoughts, Curdie was well assured that he would rather doubt his own eyes than his wife's testimony.

There were no others to whom he could have talked about it. The miners were a mingled company — some good, some not so good, some rather bad – none of them so bad or so good as they might have been; Curdie liked most of them, and was a favourite with all; but they knew very little about the upper world, and what might or might not take place there. They knew silver from copper ore; they understood the underground ways of things, and they could look very wise with their lanterns in their hands searching after this or that sign of ore, or for some mark to guide their way in the hollows of the earth; but as to great-great-grandmothers, they would have mocked Curdie all the rest of his life for the absurdity of not being absolutely certain that the solemn belief of his father and mother was nothing but ridiculous nonsense. Why, to them the very word 'great-great-grandmother' would have been a week's laughter! I am not sure that they were able quite to believe there were such persons as great-great-grandmothers; they had never seen one.

They were not companions to give the best of help toward progress, and as Curdie grew, he grew at this time faster in body than in mind – with the usual consequence, that he was getting rather stupid – one of the chief signs of which was that he believed less and less in things he had never seen. At the same time I do not think he was ever so stupid as to imagine that this was a sign of superior faculty and strength of mind. Still, he was becoming more and more a miner, and less and less a man of the upper world where the wind blew. On his way to and from the mine he took less and less notice of bees and butterflies, moths and dragonflies, the brooks and the clouds. He was gradually changing into a commonplace man.

There is this difference between the growth of some human beings and that of others: in the one case it is a continuous dying, in the other a continuous resurrection. One of the latter sort comes at length to know at once whether a thing is true the moment it comes before him; one of the former class grows more and more afraid of being taken in, so afraid of it that he takes himself in altogether, and comes at length to believe in nothing but his dinner: to be sure of a thing with him is to have it between his teeth.

Curdie was not in a very good way, then, at that time. His father and mother had, it is true, no fault to find with him — and yet — and yet — neither of them was ready to sing when the thought of him came up. There must be something wrong when a mother catches herself sighing over the time when her boy was in petticoats, or a father looks sad when he thinks how he used to carry him on his shoulder. The boy should enclose and keep, as his life, the old child at the heart of him, and never let it go. He must still, to be a right man, be his mother's darling, and more, his father's pride, and more. The child is not meant to die, but to be forever freshborn.

Curdie had made himself a bow and some arrows, and was teaching himself to shoot with them. One evening in the early summer, as he was walking home from the mine with them in his hand, a light flashed across his eyes. He looked, and there was a snow-white pigeon settling on a rock in front of him, in the red light of the level sun. There it fell at once to work with one of its wings, in which a feather or two had got some sprays twisted, causing a certain roughness unpleasant to the fastidious creature of the air.

It was indeed a lovely being, and Curdie thought how happy it must be flitting through the air with a flash — a live bolt of light. For a moment he became so one with the bird that he seemed to feel both its bill ands feathers, as the one adjusted the other to fly again, and his heart swelled with the pleasure of its involuntary sympathy. Another moment and it would have been aloft in the waves of rosy light — it was just bending its little legs to spring: that moment it fell on the path broken-winged and bleeding from Curdie's cruel arrow.

With a gush of pride at his skill, and pleasure at his success, he ran to pick up his prey. I must say for him he picked it up gently — perhaps it was the beginning of his repentance. But when he had the white thing in his hands — its whiteness stained with another red than that of the sunset flood in which it had been revelling — ah God! who knows the joy of a bird, the ectasy of a creature that has neither storehouse nor barn! — when he held it, I say, in his victorious hands, the winged thing looked up in his face — and with such eyes! asking what was the matter, and where the red sun had gone, and the clouds, and the wind of its flight. Then they closed, but to open again presently, with the same questions in them. And as they closed and opened, their look was fixed on his. It did not once flutter or try to get away; it only throbbed and bled and looked at him. Curdie's heart began to grow very large in his bosom. What could it mean? It was nothing but a pigeon, and why should he not kill a pigeon? But the fact was that not till this very moment had he ever known what a pigeon was. A good many discoveries of a similar kind have to be made by most of us. Once more it opened its eyes — then closed them again, and its throbbing ceased. Curdie gave a sob: its last look reminded him of the princess — he did not know why. He remembered how hard he had laboured to set her beyond danger, and yet what dangers she had had to encounter for his sake: they had been saviours to each other — and what had he done now? He had stopped saving, and had begun killing! What had he been sent into the world for? Surely not to be a death to its joy and loveliness. He had done the thing that was contrary to gladness; he was a destroyer! He was not the Curdie he had been meant to be!

Then the underground waters gushed from the boy's heart. And with the tears came the remembrance that a white pigeon, just before the princess went away with her father, came from somewhere – yes, from the grandmother's lamp and flew round the king and Irene and himself, and then flew away: this might be that very pigeon! Horrible to think! And if it wasn't, yet it was a white pigeon, the same as this. And if she kept a great many pigeons – and white ones, as Irene had told him, then whose pigeon could he have killed but the grand old princess's?

Suddenly everything round about him seemed against him. The red sunset stung him; the rocks frowned at him; the sweet wind that had been laving his face as he walked up the hill dropped – as if he wasn't fit to be kissed any more. Was the whole world going to cast him out? Would he have to stand there forever, not knowing what to do, with the dead pigeon in his hand? Things looked bad indeed. Was the whole world going to make a work about a pigeon – a white pigeon?

The sun went down. Great clouds gathered over the west, and shortened the twilight. The wind gave a howl, and then lay down again. The clouds gathered thicker. Then came a rumbling. He thought it was thunder. It was a rock that fell inside the mountain. A goat ran past him down the hill, followed by a dog sent to fetch him home. He thought they wer goblin creatures, and trembled. He used to despise them. And still he held the dead pigeon tenderly in his hand.

It grew darker and darker. An evil something began to move in his heart. 'What a fool I am!' he said to himself. Then he grew angry, and was just going to throw the bird from him and whistle, when a brightness shone all round him. He lifted his eyes, and saw a great globe of light — like silver at the hottest heat: he had once seen silver run from the furnace. It shone from somewhere above the roofs of the castle: it must be the great old princess's moon! How could she be there? Of course she was not there! He had asked the whole household, and nobody knew anything about her or her globe either. It couldn't be! And yet what did that signify, when there was the white globe shining, and here was the dead white bird in his hand? That moment the pigeon gave a little flutter. '*It's not dead!*' cried Curdie, almost with a shriek. The same instant he was running full speed toward the castle, never letting his heels down, lest he should shake the poor, wounded bird.

CHAPTER THREE

The Mistress of the Silver Moon

WHEN Curdie reached the castle, and ran into the little garden in front of it, there stood the door wide open. This was as he had hoped, for what could he have said if he had had to knock at it? Those whose business it is to open doors, so often mistake and shut them! But the woman now in charge often puzzled herself greatly to account for the strange fact that however often she shut the door, which, like the rest, she took a great deal of unnecessary trouble to do, she was certain, the next time she went to it, to find it open. I speak now of the great front door, of course: the back door she as persistently kept wide: if people *could* only go in by that, she said, she would then know what sort they were, and what they wanted. But she would neither have known what sort Curdie was, nor what he wanted, and would assuredly have denied him admitance, for she knew nothing of who was in the tower. So the front door was left open for him, and in he walked.

But where to go next he could not tell. It was not quite dark: a dull, shineless twilight filled the place. All he knew was that he must go up, and that proved enough for the present, for there he saw the great staircase rising before him. When he reached the top of it, he knew there must be more stairs yet, for he could not be near the top of the tower. Indeed by the situation of the stairs, he must be a good way from the tower itself. But those who work well in the depths more easily understand the heights, for indeed in their true nature they are one and the same; miners are in mountains; and Curdie, from knowing the ways of the king's mines, and being able to calculate his whereabouts in them, was now able to find his way about the king's house. He knew its outside perfectly, and now his business was to get his notion of the inside right with the outside.

So he shut his eyes and made a picture of the outside of it in his mind. Then he came in at the door of the picture, and yet kept the picture before him all the time – for you can do that kind of thing in your mind – and took every turn of the stair over again, always watching to remember, every time he turned his face, how the tower lay, and then when he came to himself at the top where he stood, he knew exactly where it was, and walked at once in the right direction.

On his way, however, he came to another stair, and up that he went, of course, watching still at every turn how the tower must lie. At the top of this stair was yet another – they were the stairs up which the princess ran when first, without knowing it, she was on her way to find her great-great-grandmother. At the top of the second stair he could go no farther, and must therefore set out again to find the tower, which, as it rose far above the rest of the house, must have the last of its stairs inside itself.

Having watched every turn to the very last, he still knew quite well in what direction he must go to find it, so he left the stair and went down a passage that led, if not exactly toward it, yet nearer it. This passage was rather dark, for it was very long, with only one window at the end, and although there were doors on both sides of it, they were all shut. At the distant window glimmered the chill east, with a few feeble stars in it, and its light was dreary and old, growing brown, and looking as if it were thinking about the day that was just gone. Presently he turned into another passage, which also had a window at the end of it; and in at that window shone all that was left of the sunset, just a few ashes, with here and there a little touch of warmth: it was nearly as sad as the east, only there was one difference – it was very plainly thinking of tomorrow.

But at present Curdie had nothing to do with today or tomorrow; his business was with the bird, and the tower where dwelt the grand old princess to whom it belonged. So he kept on his way, still eastward, and came to yet another passage, which brought him to a door. He was afraid to open it without first knocking. He knocked, but heard no answer. He was answered nevertheless; for the door gently opened, and there was a narrow stair – and so steep that, big lad as he was, he, too, like the Princess Irene before him, found his hands needful for the climbing. And it was a long climb, but he reached the top at last – a little landing, with a door in front and one on each side. Which should he knock at?

As he hesitated, he heard the noise of a spinning wheel. He knew it at once, because his mother's spinning wheel had been his governess long ago, and still taught him things. It was the spinning wheel that first taught him to make verses, and to sing, and to think whether all was right inside him; or at least it had helped him in all these things. Hence it was no wonder he should know a spinning wheel when he heard it sing – even although as the bird of paradise to other birds was the song of that wheel to the song of his mother's. He stood listening, so entranced that he forgot to knock, and the wheel went on and on, spinning in his brain songs and tales and rhymes, till he was almost asleep as well as dreaming, for sleep does not *always* come first. But suddenly came the thought of the poor bird, which had been lying motionless in his hand all the time, and that woke him up, and at once he knocked.

'Come in, Curdie,' said a voice.

Curdie shook. It was getting rather awful. The heart that had never much heeded any army of goblins trembled at the soft word of invitation. But then there was the red-spotted white thing in his hand! He dared not hesitate, though. Gently he opened the door through which the sound came, and what did he see? Nothing at first – except indeed a great sloping shaft of moonlight that came in at a high window, and rested on the floor. He stood and stared at it, forgetting to shut the door.

'Why don't you come in, Curdie?' said the voice. 'Did you never see moonlight before?'

'Never without a moon,' answered Curdie, in a trembling tone, but gathering courage.

'Certainly not,' returned the voice, which was thin and quavering: '*I* never saw moonlight without a moon.'

'But there's no moon outside,' said Curdie.

'Ah! but you're inside now,' said the voice.

The answer did not satisfy Curdie; but the voice went on.

'There are more moons than you know of, Curdie. Where there is one sun there are many moons – and of many sorts. Come in and look out of my window, and you will soon satisfy yourself that there is a moon looking in at it.'

The gentleness of the voice made Curdie remember his manners. He shut the door, and drew a step or two nearer to the moonlight.

All the time the sound of the spinning had been going on

and on, and Curdie now caught sight of the wheel. Oh, it was such a thin, delicate thing — reminding him of a spider's web in a hedge. It stood in the middle of the moonlight, and it seemed as if the moonlight had nearly melted it away. A step nearer, he saw, with a start, two little hands at work with it. And then at last, in the shadow on the other side of the moonlight which came like a river between, he saw the form to which the hands belonged: a small withered creature, so old that no age would have seemed too great to write under her picture, seated on a stool beyond the spinning wheel, which looked very large beside her, but, as I said, very thin, like a long-legged spider holding up its own web, which was the round wheel itself. She sat crumpled together, a filmy thing that it seemed a puff would blow away, more like the body of a fly the big spider had sucked empty and left hanging in his web, than anything else I can think of.

When Curdie saw her, he stood still again, a good deal in wonder, a very little in reverence, a little in doubt, and, I must add, a little in amusement at the odd look of the old marvel. Her grey hair mixed with the moonlight so that he could not tell where the one began and the other ended. Her crooked back bent forward over her chest, her shoulders nearly swallowed up her head between them, and her two little hands were just like the grey claws of a hen, scratching at the thread, which to Curdie was of course invisible across the moonlight. Indeed Curdie laughed within himself, just a little, at the sight; and when he thought of how the princess used to talk about her huge, great, old grandmother, he laughed more. But that moment the little lady leaned forward into the moonlight, and Curdie caught a glimpse of her eyes, and all the laugh went out of him.

'What do you come here for, Curdie?' she said, as gently as before.

Then Curdie remembered that he stood there as a culprit, and worst of all, as one who had his confession yet to make. There was no time to hesitate over it.

'Oh, ma'am! See here,' he said, and advanced a step or two, holding out the pigeon.

'What have you got there?' she asked.

Again Curdie advanced a few steps, and held out his hand with the pigeon, that she might see what it was, into the moonlight. The moment the rays fell upon it the pigeon gave a faint flutter. The old lady put out her old hands and took it, and held it to her bosom, and rocked it, murmuring over it as if it were a sick baby.

When Curdie saw how distressed she was he grew sorrier still, and said:

'I didn't mean to do any harm, ma'am, I didn't think of its being yours.'

'Ah, Curdie! If it weren't mine, what would become of it now?' she returned. 'You say you didn't mean any harm: did you mean any good, Curdie?'

'No,' answered Curdie.

'Remember, then, that whoever does not mean good is always in danger of harm. But I try to give everybody fair play; and those that are in the wrong are in far more need of it always than those who are in the right: they can afford to do without. Therefore I say for you that when you shot that arrow you did not know what a pigeon is. Now that you do know, your are sorry. It is very dangerous to do things you don't know about.'

'But, please ma'am – I don't mean to be rude or to contra-

dict you,' said Curdie, 'but if a body was never to do anything but what he knew to be good, he would have to live half
his time doing nothing.'

'There you are much mistaken,' said the old quavering
voice. 'How little you must have thought! Why, you don't
seem even to know the good of the things you are constantly
doing. Now don't mistake me. I don't mean you are good for
doing them. It is a good thing to eat your breakfast, but you
don't fancy it's very good of you to do it. The thing is good –
not you.'

Curdie laughed.

'There are a great many more good things than bad things
to do. Now tell me what bad thing you have done today
besides this sore hurt to my little white friend.'

While she talked Curdie had sunk into a sort of reverie, in
which he hardly knew whether it was the old lady or his own
heart that spoke. And when she asked him that question, he
was at first much inclined to consider himself a very good
fellow on the whole. 'I really don't think I did anything else
that was very bad all day,' he said to himself. But at the same
time he could not honestly feel that he was worth standing up
for. All at once a light seemed to break in upon his mind, and
he woke up and there was the withered little atomy of the old
lady on the other side of the moonlight, and there was the
spinning wheel singing on and on in the middle of it!

'I know now, ma'am; I understand now,' he said. 'Thank
you, ma'am, for spinning it into me with your wheel. I see
now that I have been doing wrong the whole day, and such a
many days besides! Indeed, I don't know when I ever did
right, and yet it seems as if I had done right some time and had
forgotten how. When I killed your bird I did not know I was

doing wrong, just because I was always doing wrong, and the wrong had soaked all through me.'

'What wrong were you doing all day, Curdie? It is better to come to the point, you know,' said the old lady, and her voice was gentler even than before.

'I was doing the wrong of never wanting or trying to be better. And now I see that I have been letting things go as they would for a long time. Whatever came into my head I did, and whatever didn't come into my head I didn't do. I never sent anything away, and never looked out for anything to come. I haven't been attending to my mother – or my father either. And now I think of it, I know I have often seen them looking troubled, and I have never asked them what was the matter. And now I see, too, that I did not ask because I suspected it had something to do with me and my behaviour, and didn't want to hear the truth. And I know I have been grumbling at work, and doing a hundred other things wrong.'

'You have got it, Curdie,' said the old lady, in a voice that sounded almost as if she had been crying. 'When people don't care to be better they must be doing everything wrong. I am so glad you shot my bird!'

'Ma'am!' exclaimed Curdie. 'How *can* you be?'

'Because it has brought you to see what sort you were when you did it, and what sort you will grow to be again, only worse, if you don't mind. Now that you are sorry, my poor bird will be better. Look up, my dovey.'

The pigeon gave a flutter, and spread out one of its red-spotted wings across the old woman's bosom.

'I will mend the little angel,' she said, 'and in a week or two it will be flying again. So you may ease your heart about the pigeon.'

'Oh, thank you! Thank you!' cried Curdie. 'I don't know how to thank you.'

'Then I will tell you. There is only one way I care for. Do better, and grow better, and be better. And never kill anything without a good reason for it.'

'Ma'am, I will go and fetch my bow and arrows, and you shall burn them yourself.'

'I have no fire that would burn your bow and arrows, Curdie.'

'Then I promise you to burn them all under my mother's porridge pot tomorrow morning.'

'No, no, Curdie. Keep them, and practice with them every day, and grow a good shot. There are plenty of bad things that want killing, and a day will come when they will prove useful. But I must see first whether you will do as I tell you.'

'That I will!' said Curdie. 'What is it, ma'am?'

'Only something not to do,' answered the old lady; 'If you should hear anyone speak about me, never to laugh or make fun of me.'

'Oh, ma'am!' exclaimed Curdie, shocked that she should think such a request needful.

'Stop, stop,' she went on. 'People hereabout sometimes tell very odd and in fact ridiculous stories of an old woman who watches what is going on, and occasionally interferes. They mean me, though what they say is often great nonsense. Now what I want of you is not to laugh, or side with them in any way; because they will take that to mean that you don't believe there is any such person a bit more than they do. Now that would not be the case — would it, Curdie?'

'No, indeed, ma'am. I've seen you.'

The old woman smiled very oddly.

'Yes, you've seen me,' she said. 'But mind,' she continued, 'I don't want you to say anything – only to hold your tongue, and not seem to side with them.'

'That will be easy,' said Curdie, 'now that I've seen you with my very own eyes, ma'am.'

'Not so easy as you think, perhaps,' said the old lady, with another curious smile. 'I want to be your friend,' she added after a little pause, 'but I don't quite know yet whether you will let me.'

'Indeed I will, ma'am,' said Curdie.

'That is for me to find out,' she rejoined, with yet another strange smile. 'In the meantime all I can say is, come to me again when you find yourself in any trouble, and I will see what I can do for you – only the *canning* depends on yourself. I am greatly pleased with you for bringing me my pigeon, doing your best to set right what you had set wrong.'

As she spoke she held out her hand to him, and when he took it she made use of his to help herself up from her stool, and – when or how it came about, Curdie could not tell – the same instant she stood before him a tall, strong woman – plainly very old, but as grand as she was old, and only *rather* severe-looking. Every trace of the decrepitude and withered-ness she showed as she hovered like a film about her wheel, had vanished. Her hair was very white, but it hung about her head in great plenty, and shone like silver in the moonlight. Straight as a pillar she stood before the astonished boy, and the wounded bird had now spread out both its wings across her bosom, like some great mystical ornament of frosted silver.

'Oh, now I can never forget you!' cried Curdie. 'I see now what you really are!'

'Did I not tell you the truth when I sat at my wheel?' said

the old lady.

'Yes, ma'am,' answered Curdie.

'I can do no more than tell you the truth now,' she rejoined. 'It is a bad thing indeed to forget one who has told us the truth. Now go.'

Curdie obeyed, and took a few steps toward the door.

'Please, ma'am — what am I to call you?' he was going to say; but when he turned to speak, he saw nobody. Whether she was there or not he could not tell, however, for the moonlight had vanished, and the room was utterly dark. A great fear, such as he had never before known, came upon him, and almost overwhelmed him. He groped his way to the door, and crawled down the stair — in doubt and anxiety as to how he should find his way out of the house in the dark. And the stair seemed ever so much longer than when he came up. Nor was that any wonder, for down and down he went, until at length his foot struck a door, and when he rose and opened it, he found himself under the starry, moonless sky at the foot of the tower.

He soon discovered the way out of the garden, with which he had some acquaintance already, and in a few minutes was climbing the mountain with a solemn and cheerful heart. It was rather dark, but he knew the way well. As he passed the rock from which the poor pigeon fell wounded with his arrow, a great joy filled his heart at the thought that he was delivered from the blood of the little bird, and he ran the next hundred yards at full speed up the hill. Some dark shadows passed him: he did not even care to think what they were, but let them run. When he reached home, he found his father and mother waiting supper for him.

CHAPTER FOUR

Curdie's Father and Mother

THE eyes of the fathers and mothers are quick to read their children's looks, and when Curdie entered the cottage, his parents saw at once that something unusual had taken place. When he said to his mother, 'I beg your pardon for being so late,' there was something in the tone beyond the politeness that went to her heart, for it seemed to come from the place where all lovely things were born before they began to grow in this world. When he set his father's chair to the table, an attention he had not shown him for a long time, Peter thanked him with more gratitude than the boy had ever yet felt in all his life. It was a small thing to do for the man who had been serving him since ever he was born, but I suspect there is nothing a man can be so grateful for as that to which he has the most right.

There was a change upon Curdie, and father and mother felt there must be something to account for it, and therefore were pretty sure he had something to tell them. For when a child's heart is *all* right, it is not likely he will want to keep anything from his parents. But the story of the evening was too solemn for Curdie to come out with all at once. He must wait until they had had their porridge, and the affairs of this

35

world were over for the day.

But when they were seated on the grassy bank of the brook that went so sweetly blundering over the great stones of its rocky channel, for the whole meadow lay on the top of a huge rock, then he felt that the right hour had come for sharing with them the wonderful things that had come to him. It was perhaps the loveliest of all hours in the year. The summer was young and soft, and this was the warmest evening they had yet had — dusky, dark even below, while above, the stars were bright and large and sharp in the blackest blue sky. The night came close around them, clasping them in one universal arm of love, and although it neither spoke nor smiled, seemed all eye and ear, seemed to see and hear and know everything they said and did. It is a way the night has sometimes, and there is a reason for it. The only sound was that of the brook, for there was no wind, and no trees for it to make its music upon if there had been, for the cottage was high up on the mountain, on a great shoulder of stone where trees would not grow.

There, to the accompaniment of the water, as it hurried down to the valley and the sea, talking busily of a thousand true things which it could not understand, Curdie told his tale, outside and in, to his father and mother. What a world had slipped in between the mouth of the mine and his mother's cottage! Neither of them said a word until he had ended.

'Now what am I to make of it, Mother. It's so strange!' he said, and stopped.

'It's easy enough to see what Curdie has got to make of it — isn't it, Peter,' said the good woman, turning her face toward all she could see of her husband's.

'It seems so to me,' answered Peter, with a smile which only the night saw, but his wife felt in the tone of his words. They were the happiest couple in that country, because they always understood each other, and that was because they always meant the same thing, and that was because they always loved what was fair and true and right better, not than anything else, but than everything else put together.

'Then will you tell Curdie?' said she.

'You can talk best, Joan,' said he. 'You tell him, I will listen – and learn how to say what I think,' he added.

'*I*,' said Curdie, 'don't know what to think.'

'It does not matter so much,' said his mother. 'If only you know what to make of a thing, you'll know soon enough what to think of it. Now I needn't tell you, surely, Curdie, what you've got to do with this?'

'I suppose you mean, Mother,' answered Curdie, 'that I must do as the old lady told me?'

'That is what I mean: what else could it be? Am I not right, Peter?'

'Quite right, Joan,' answered Peter, 'so far as my judgement goes. It is a very strange story, but you see the question is not about believing it, for Curdie knows what came to him.'

'And you remember, Curdie,' said his mother, 'that when the princess took you up that tower once before, and there talked to her great-great-grandmother, you came home quite angry with her, and said there was nothing in the place but an old tub, a heap of straw – oh, I remember your inventory quite well! – an old tub, a heap of straw, a withered apple, and a sunbeam. According to your eyes, that was all there was in the great, old, musty garret. But now you have had a glimpse of the old princess herself!'

'Yes, Mother, I *did* see her – or if I didn't –' said Curdie very thoughtfully – then began again. 'The hardest thing to believe, though I saw it with my own eyes, was when the thin, filmy creature that seemed almost to float about in the moonlight like a bit of the silver paper they put over pictures, or like a handkerchief made of spider threads, took my hand, and rose up. She was taller and stronger than you, Mother, ever so much! – at least, she looked so.'

'And most certainly was so, Curdie, if she looked so,' said Mrs Peterson.

'Well, I confess,' returned her son, 'that one thing, if there were no other, would make me doubt whether I was not dreaming, after all, wide awake though I fancied myself to be.'

'Of course,' answered his mother, 'it is not for me to say whether you were dreaming or not if you are doubtful of it yourself; but it doesn't make me think I am dreaming when in the summer I hold in my hand the bunch of sweet peas that make my heart glad with their colour and scent, and remember the dry, withered-looking little thing I dibbled into the hole in the same spot in the spring. I only think how wonderful and lovely it all is. It seems just as full of reason as it is of wonder. How it is done I can't tell, only there it is! And there is this in it, too, Curdie – of which you would not be so ready to think – that when you come home to your father and mother, and they find you behaving more like a dear, good son than you have behaved for a long time, they at least are not likely to think you were only dreaming.'

'Still,' said Curdie, looking a little ashamed. 'I might have dreamed my duty.'

'Then dream often, my son; for there must then be more truth in your dreams than in your waking thoughts. But however any of these things may be, this one point remains certain: there can be no harm in doing as she told you. And, indeed, until you are sure there is no such person, you are bound to do it, for you promised.'

'It seems to me,' said his father, 'that if a lady comes to you in a dream, Curdie, and tells you not to talk about her when you wake, the least you can do is to hold your tongue.'

'True, Father! Yes, Mother, I'll do it,' said Curdie.

Then they went to bed, and sleep, which is the night of the soul, next took them in its arms and made them well.

CHAPTER FIVE

The Miners

IT much increased Curdie's feeling of the strangeness of the whole affair, that, the next morning, when they were at work in the mine, the party of which he and his father were two, just as if they had known what had happened to him the night before, began talking about all manner of wonderful tales that were abroad in the country, chiefly of course, those connected with the mines, and the mountains in which they lay. Their wives and mothers and grandmothers were their chief authorities. For when they sat by their firesides they heard their wives telling their children the selfsame tales, with little differences, and here and there one they had not heard before, which they had heard their mothers and grandmothers tell in one or other of the same cottages.

At length they came to speak of a certain strange being they called Old Mother Wotherwop. Some said their wives had seen her. It appeared as they talked that not one had seen her more than once. Some of their mothers and grandmothers, however, had seen her also, and they all had told them tales about her when they were children. They said she could take any shape she liked, but that in reality she was a withered old woman, so old and so withered that she was as thin as a sieve with a lamp behind it; that she was never seen except at night, and when something terrible had taken place, or was going to take place — such as the falling in of the roof of a mine, or the breaking out of water in it.

She had more than once been seen — it was always at night — beside some well, sitting on the brink of it, and leaning over and stirring it with her forefinger, which was six times as long as any of the rest. And whoever for months after drank of that well was sure to be ill. To this, one of them, however, added that he remembered his mother saying that whoever in bad health drank of the well was sure to get better. But the majority agreed that the former was the right version of the story — for was she not a witch, an old hating witch, whose delight was to do mischief? One said he had heard that she took the shape of a young woman sometimes, as beautiful as an angel, and then was most dangerous of all, for she struck every man who looked upon her stone-blind.

Peter ventured the question whether she might not as likely be an angel that took the form of an old woman, as an old woman that took the form of an angel. But nobody except Curdie, who was holding his peace with all his might, saw any sense in the question. They said an old woman might be very glad to make herself look like a young one, but who ever heard of a young and beautiful one making herself look old and ugly?

Peter asked why they were so much more ready to believe the bad that was said of her than the good. They answered, because she was bad. He asked why they believed her to be bad, and they answered, because she did bad things. When he asked how they knew that, they said, because she was a bad creature. Even if they didn't know it, they said, a woman like

41

that was so much more likely to be bad than good. Why did she go about at night? Why did she appear only now and then, and on such occasions? One went on to tell how one night when his grandfather had been having a jolly time of it with his friends in the market town, she had served him so upon his way home that the poor man never drank a drop of anything stronger than water after it to the day of his death. She dragged him into a bog, and tumbled him up and down in it till he was nearly dead.

'I suppose that was her way of teaching him what a good thing water was,' said Peter; but the man, who liked strong drink, did not see the joke.

'They do say,' said another, 'that she has lived in the old house over there ever since the little princess left it. They say, too, that the housekeeper knows all about it, and is hand and glove with the old witch. I don't doubt they have many a nice airing together on broomsticks. But I don't doubt either it's all nonsense, and there's no such person at all.'

'When our cow died,' said another, 'she was seen going round and round the cowhouse the same night. To be sure she left a fine calf behind her – I mean the cow did, not the witch. I wonder she didn't kill that, too, for she'll be a far finer cow than ever her mother was.'

'My old woman came upon her one night, not long before the water broke out in the mine, sitting on a stone on the hillside with a whole congregation of cobs about her. When they saw my wife they all scampered off as fast as they could run, and where the witch was sitting was nothing to be seen but a withered bracken bush. I made no doubt myself she was putting them up to it.'

And so they went on with one foolish tale after another,

while Peter put in a word now and then, and Curdie diligently held his peace. But his silence at last drew attention upon it, and one of them said:

'Come, young Curdie, what are you thinking of?'

'How do you know I'm thinking of anything?' asked Curdie.

'Because you're not saying anything.'

'Does it follow then that, as you are saying so much, you're not thinking at all?' said Curdie.

'I know what he's thinking,' said one who had not yet spoken; 'he's thinking what a set of fools you are to talk such rubbish; as if ever there was or could be such an old woman as you say! I'm sure Curdie knows better than all that comes to.'

'I think,' said Curdie, 'it would be better that he who says anything about her should be quite sure it is true, lest she should hear him, and not like to be slandered.'

'But would she like it any better if it were true?' said the same man. 'If she is what they say – I don't know – but I never knew a man that wouldn't go in a rage to be called the very thing he was.'

'If bad things were true of her, and I *knew* it,' said Curdie, 'I would not hesitate to say them, for I will never give in to being afraid of anything that's bad. I suspect that the things they tell, however, if we knew all about them, would turn out to have nothing but good in them; and I won't say a word more for fear I should say something that mightn't be to her mind.'

They all burst into a loud laugh.

'Hear the parson!' they cried. 'He believes in the witch! Ha! ha!'

'He's afraid of her!'

'And says all she does is good!'

'He wants to make friends with her, that she may help him to find the silver ore.'

'Give me my own eyes and a good divining rod before all the witches in the world! And so I'd advise you too, Master Curdie; that is, when your eyes have grown to be worth anything, and you have learned to cut the hazel fork.'

Thus they all mocked and jeered at him, but he did his best to keep his temper and go quietly on with his work. He got as close to his father as he could, however, for that helped him to bear it. As soon as they were tired of laughing and mocking, Curdie was friendly with them, and long before their midday meal all between them was as it had been.

But when the evening came, Peter and Curdie felt that they would rather walk home together without other company, and therefore lingered behind when the rest of the men left the mine.

CHAPTER SIX

The Emerald

FATHER and son had seated themselves on a projecting piece of rock at a corner where three galleries met – the one they had come along from their work, one to the right leading out of the mountain, and the other to the left leading far into a portion of it which had been long disused. Since the inundation caused by the goblins, it had indeed been rendered impassable by the settlement of a quantity of the water, forming a small but very deep lake, in a part where there was a considerable descent.

They had just risen and were turning to the right, when a gleam caught their eyes, and made them look along the whole gallery. Far up they saw a pale green light, whence issuing they could not tell, about halfway between floor and roof of the passage. They saw nothing but the light, which was like a large star, with a point of darker colour yet brighter radiance in the heart of it, whence the rest of the light shot out in rays that faded toward the ends until they vanished. It shed hardly any light around it, although in itself it was so bright as to sting the eyes that beheld it. Wonderful stories had from ages gone been current in the mines about certain magic gems which gave out light of themselves, and this light looked just like what might be supposed to shoot from the heart of such a gem. They went up the old gallery to find out what it could be.

To their surprise they found, however, that, after going some distance, they were no nearer to it, so far as they could judge, than when they started. It did not seem to move, and yet they moving did not approach it. Still they perservered, for it was far too wonderful a thing to lose sight of, so long as they could keep it. At length they drew near the hollow where the water lay, and still were no nearer the light. Where they expected to be stopped by the water, however, water was none: something had taken place in some part of the mine that had drained it off, and the gallery lay open as in former times.

And now, to their surprise, the light, instead of being in front of them, was shining at the same distance to the right, where they did not know there was any passage at all. Then they discovered, by the light of the lanterns they carried, that there the water had broken through, and made an entrance to a part of the mountain of which Peter knew nothing. But they were hardly well into it, still following the light, before Curdie thought he recognized some of the passages he had so often gone through when he was watching the goblins.

After they had advanced a long way, with many turnings, now to the right, now to the left, all at once their eyes seemed to come suddenly to themselves, and they became aware that the light which they had taken to be a great way from them was in reality almost within reach of their hands. The same instant it began to grow larger and thinner, the point of light grew dim as it spread, the greenness melted away, and in a moment or two, instead of the star, a dark, dark and yet luminous face was looking at them with living eyes. And Curdie felt a great awe swell up in his heart, for he thought he had seen those eyes before.

'I see you know me, Curdie,' said a voice.

'If your eyes are you, ma'am, then I know you,' said Curdie.
'But I never saw your face before.'

'Yes, you have seen it, Curdie,' said the voice.

And with that the darkness of its complexion melted away,
and down from the face dawned out the form that belonged to it,
until at last Curdie and his father beheld a lady, beautiful exceed-
ingly, dressed in something pale green, like velvet, over which
her hair fell in cataracts of a rich golden colour. It looked as if it
were pouring down from her head, and, like the water of the
Dustbrook, vanishing in a golden vapour ere it reached the
floor. It came flowing from under the edge of a coronet of gold,
set with alternated pearls and emeralds. In front of the crown
was a great emerald, which looked somehow as if out of it had
come the light they had followed. There was no ornament else
about her, except on her slippers, which were one mass of
gleaming emeralds, of various shades of green, all mingling
lovelily like the waving of grass in the wind and sun. She
looked about five-and-twenty years old. And for all the
difference, Curdie knew somehow or other, he could not
have told how, that the face before him was that of the old
princess, Irene's great-great-grandmother.

By this time all around them had grown light, and now first
they could see where they were. They stood in a great splendid
cavern, which Curdie recognized as that in which the goblins
held their state assemblies. But, strange to tell, the light by which
they saw came streaming, sparkling, and shooting from stones of
many colours in the sides and roof and floor of the cavern—stones
of all the colours of the rainbow, and many more. It was a
glorious sight—the whole rugged place flashing with colours—
in one spot a great light of deep carbuncular red, in another of
sapphirine blue, in another of topaz yellow; while here and

there were groups of stones of all hues and sizes, and again nebulous spaces of thousands of tiniest spots of brilliancy of every conceivable shade. Sometimes the colours ran together, and made a little river or lake of lambent, interfusing, and changing tints, which, by their variegation, seemed to imitate the flowing of water, or waves made by the wind.

Curdie would have gazed entranced, but that all the beauty of the cavern, yes, of all he knew of the whole creation, seemed gathered in one centre of harmony and loveliness in the person of the ancient lady who stood before him in the very summer of beauty and strength. Turning from the first glance at the circumfulgent splendour, it dwindled into nothing as he looked again at the lady. Nothing flashed or glowed or shone about her, and yet it was with a prevision of the truth that he said:

'I was here once before, ma'am.'

'I know that, Curdie,' she replied.

'The place was full of torches, and the walls gleamed, but nothing as they do now, and there is no light in the place.'

'You want to know where the light comes from?' she said, smiling.

'Yes, ma'am.'

'Then see: I will go out of the cavern. Do not be afraid, but watch.'

She went slowly out. The moment she turned her back to go, the light began to pale and fade; the moment she was out of their sight the place was black as night, save that now the smoky yellow-red of their lamps, which they thought had gone out long ago, cast a dusky glimmer around them.

CHAPTER SEVEN

What *Is* in a Name?

FOR a time that seemed to them long, the two men stood waiting, while still the Mother of Light did not return. So long was she absent that they began to grow anxious: how were they to find their way from natural hollows of the mountain crossed by goblin paths, if their lamps should go out? To spend the night there would mean to sit and wait until an earthquake rent the mountain, or the earth herself fell back into the smelting furnace of the sun whence she had issued — for it was all night and no faintest dawn in the bosom of the world.

So long did they wait unrevisited, that, had there not been two of them, either would at length have concluded the vision a home-born product of his own seething brain. And their lamps *were* going out, for they grew redder and smokier! But they did not lose courage, for there is a kind of capillary attraction in the facing of two souls, that lifts faith quite beyond the level to which either could raise it alone: they knew that they had seen the lady of emeralds, and it was to give them their own desire that she had gone from them, and neither would yield for a moment to the half doubts and half dreads that awoke in his heart.

And still she who with her absence darkened their air did not return. They grew weary, and sat down on the rocky floor, for wait they would — indeed, wait they must. Each set his lamp by his knee, and watched it die. Slowly it sank, dulled, looked lazy and stupid. But ever as it sank and dulled, the image in his mind of the Lady of Light grew stronger and clearer. Together the two lamps panted and shuddered. First one, then the other went out, leaving for a moment a great, red, evil-smelling snuff. Then all was the blackness of darkness up to their very hearts and everywhere around them. Was it? No. Far away — it looked miles away — shone one minute faint point of green light — where, who could tell? They only knew that it shone. It grew larger, and seemed to draw nearer, until at last, as they watched with speechless delight and expectation, it seemed once more within reach of an outstretched hand. Then it spread and melted away as before, and there were eyes — and a face — and a lovely form — and lo! the whole cavern blazing with lights innumerable, and gorgeous, yet soft and interfused — so blended, indeed, that the eye had to search and see in order to separate distinct spots of special colour.

The moment they saw the speck in the vast distance they had risen and stood on their feet. When it came nearer they bowed their heads. Yet now they looked with fearless eyes, for the woman that was old yet young was a joy to see, and filled their hearts with reverent delight. She turned first to Peter.

'I have known you long.' she said. 'I have met you going to and from the mine, and seen you working in it for the last forty years.'

'How should it be, madam, that a grand lady like you should take notice of a poor man like me?' said Peter, humbly, but more foolishly than he could then have understood.

'I am poor as well as rich,' said she, 'I, too, work for my bread, and I show myself no favour when I pay myself my own wages. Last night when you sat by the brook, and Curdie told you about my pigeon, and my spinning, and wondered whether he could believe that he had actually seen me, I heard all you said to each other. I am always about, as the miners said the other night when they talked of me as Old Mother Wotherwop.'

The lovely lady laughed, and her laugh was a lightning of delight in their souls.

'Yes,' she went on, 'you have got to thank me that you are so poor, Peter. I have seen to that, and it has done well for both you and me, my friend. Things come to the poor that can't get in at the door of the rich. Their money somehow blocks it up. It is a great privilege to be poor, Peter—one that no man ever coveted, and but a very few have sought to retain, but one that yet many have learned to prize. You must not mistake, however, and imagine it a virtue; it is but a privilege, and one also that, like other privileges, may be terribly misused. Had you been rich, my Peter, you would not have been so good as some rich men I know. And now I am going to tell you what no one knows but myself: you, Peter, and your wife both have the blood of the royal family in your veins. I have been trying to cultivate your family tree, every branch of which is known to me, and I expect Curdie to turn out a blossom on it. Therefore I have been training him for a work that must soon be done. I was near losing him, and had to send my pigeon. Had he not shot it, that would have been better; but he repented, and that shall be as good in the end.'

She turned to Curdie and smiled.

'Ma'am,' said Curdie, 'may I ask questions?'

'Why not, Curdie?'

'Because I have been told, ma'am, that nobody must ask the king questions.'

51

'The king never made that law,' she answered, with some displeasure. 'You may ask me as many as you please – that is, so long as they are sensible. Only I may take a few thousand years to answer some of them. But that's nothing. Of all things time is the cheapest.'

'Then would you mind telling me now, ma'am, for I feel very confused about it – are you the Lady of the Silver Moon?'

'Yes, Curdie; you may call me that if you like. What it means is true.'

'And now I see you dark, and clothed in green, and the mother of all the light that dwells in the stones of the earth! And up there they call you Old Mother Wotherwop! And the Princess Irene told me you were her great-great-grandmother! And you spin the spider threads, and take care of a whole people of pigeons; and you are worn to a pale shadow with old age; and are as young as anybody can be, not to be too young; and as strong, I do believe, as I am.'

The lady stooped toward a large green stone bedded in the rock of the floor, and looking like a well of grassy light in it. She laid hold of it with her fingers, broke it out, and gave it to Peter.

'There!' cried Curdie. 'I told you so. Twenty men could not have done that. And your fingers are white and smooth as any lady's in the land. I don't know what to make of it.'

'I could give you twenty names more to call me, Curdie, and not one of them would be a false one. What does it matter how many names if the person is one?'

'Ah! But it is not names only, ma'am. Look at what you were like last night, and what I see you now!'

'Shapes are only dresses, Curdie, and dresses are only names. That which is inside is the same all the time.

'But then how can all the shapes speak the truth?'

'It would want thousands more to speak the truth, Curdie; and then they could not. But there is a point I must not let you mistake about. It is one thing the shape I choose to put on, and quite another the shape that foolish talk and nursery tale may please to put upon me. Also, it is one thing what you or your father may think about me, and quite another what a foolish or bad man may see in me. For instance, if a thief were to come in here just now, he would think he saw the demon of the mine, all in green flames, come to protect her treasure, and would run like a hunted wild goat. I should be all the same, but his evil eyes would see me as I was not.'

'I think I understand,' said Curdie.

'Peter,' said the lady, turning then to him, 'you will have to give up Curdie for a little while.'

'So long as he loves us, ma'am, that will not matter – much.'

'Ah! you are right there, my friend,' said the beautiful princess.

And as she said it she put out her hand, and took the hard, horny hand of the miner in it, and held it for a moment lovingly.

'I need say no more,' she added, 'for we understand each other – you and I, Peter.'

The tears came into Peter's eyes. He bowed his head in thankfulness, and his heart was much too full to speak.

Then the great old, young, beautiful princess turned to Curdie.

'Now, Curdie, are you ready?' she said.

'Yes, ma'am,' answered Curdie.

'You do not know what for.'

'You do, ma'am. That is enough.'

'You could not have given me a better answer, or done more to prepare yourself, Curdie,' she returned, with one of her

53

radiant smiles. 'Do you think you will know me again?'

'I think so. But how can I tell what you may look like next?'

'Ah, that indeed! How can you tell? Or how could I expect you should? But those who know me *well*, know me whatever new dress or shape or name I may be in; and by and by you will have learned to do so too.'

'But if you want me to know you again, ma'am, for certain sure,' said Curdie, 'could you not give me some sign, or tell me something about you that never changes—or some other way to know you, or thing to know you by?'

'No, Curdie; that would be to keep you from knowing me. You must know me in quite another way from that. It would not be the least use to you or me either if I were to make you know me in that way. It would be but to know the sign of me—not to know me myself. It would be no better than if I were to take this emerald out of my crown and give it to you to take home with you, and you were to call it me, and talk to it as if it heard and saw and loved you. Much good that would do you, Curdie! No; you must do what you can to know me, and if you do, you will. You shall see me again—in very different circumstances from these, and, I will tell you so much, it *may* be in a very different shape. But come now, I will lead you out of this cavern; my good Joan will be getting too anxious about you. One word more: you will allow that the men knew little what they were talking about this morning, when they told all those tales of Old Mother Wotherwop; but did it occur to you to think how it was they fell to talking about me at all? It was because I came to them; I was beside them all the time they were talking about me, though they were far enough from knowing it, and had very little besides foolishness to say.'

As she spoke she turned and led the way from the cavern,

which, as if a door had been closed, sank into absolute blackness behind them. And now they saw nothing more of the lady except the green star, which again seemed a good distance in front of them, and to which they came no nearer, although following it at a quick pace through the mountain. Such was their confidence in her guidance, however, and so fearless were they in consequence, that they felt their way neither with hand nor foot, but walked straight on through the pitch-dark galleries. When at length the night of the upper world looked in at the mouth of the mine, the green light seemed to lose its way among the stars, and they saw it no more.

Out they came into the cool, blessed night. It was very late, and only starlight. To their surprise, three paces away they saw, seated upon a stone, an old country-woman, in a cloak which they took for black. When they came close up to it they saw it was red.

'Good evening!' said Peter.

'Good evening!' returned the old woman, in a voice as old as herself.

But Curdie took off his cap and said:

'I am your servant, Princess.'

The old woman replied:

'Come to me in the dove tower tomorrow night, Curdie — alone.'

'I will ma'am,' said Curdie.

So they parted, and father and son went home to wife and mother — two persons in one rich, happy woman.

CHAPTER EIGHT

Curdie's Mission

THE next night Curdie went home from the mine a little earlier than usual, to make himself tidy before going to the dove tower. The princess had not appointed an exact time for him to be there; he would go as near the time he had gone first as he could. On his way to the bottom of the hill, he met his father coming up. The sun was then down, and the warm first of the twilight filled the evening. He came rather wearily up the hill: the road, he thought, must have grown steeper in parts since he was Curdie's age. His back was to the light of the sunset, which closed him all round in a beautiful setting, and Curdie thought what a grand-looking man his father was, even when he was tired. It is greed and laziness and selfishness, not hunger or weariness or cold, that take the dignity out of a man, and make him look mean.

'Ah, Curdie! There you are!' he said, seeing his son come bounding along as if it were morning with him and not evening.

'You look tired, Father,' said Curdie.

'Yes, my boy. I'm not so young as you.'

'Nor so old as the princess,' said Curdie.

'Tell me this,' said Peter, 'why do people talk about going

downhill when they begin to get old? It seems to me that then first they begin to go uphill.'

'You looked to me, Father, when I caught sight of you, as if you had been climbing the hill all your life, and were soon to get to the top.'

'Nobody can tell when that will be,' returned Peter. 'We're so ready to think we're just at the top when it lies miles away. But I must not keep you, my boy, for you are wanted; and we shall be anxious to know what the princess says to you — that is, if she will allow you to tell us.'

'I think she will, for she knows there is nobody more to be trusted than my father and mother,' said Curdie, with pride.

And away he shot, and ran, and jumped, and seemed almost to fly down the long, winding, steep path, until he came to the gate of the king's house.

There he met an unexpected obstruction: in the open door stood the housekeeper, and she seemed to broaden herself out until she almost filled the doorway.

'So!' she said, 'it's you, is it, young man? You are the person that comes in and goes out when he pleases, and keeps running up and down my stairs without ever saying by your leave, or even wiping his shoes, and always leaves the door open! Don't you know this is my house?'

'No, I do not,' returned Curdie respectfully. 'You forget, ma'am, that it is the king's house.'

'That is all the same. The king left it to me to take care of and that you shall know!'

'Is the king dead, ma'am, that he has left it to you?' asked Curdie, half in doubt from the self-assertion of the woman.

'Insolent fellow!' exclaimed the housekeeper. 'Don't you see by my dress that I am in the king's service?'

'And am I not one of his miners?'

'Ah! that goes for nothing. I am one of his household. You are an out-of-doors labourer. You are a nobody. You carry a pickaxe. I carry the keys at my girdle. See!'

'But you must not call one a nobody to whom the king has spoken,' said Curdie.

'Go along with you!' cried the housekeeper, and would have shut the door in his face, had she not been afraid that when she stepped back he would step in ere she could get it in motion, for it was very heavy and always seemed unwilling to shut. Curdie came a pace nearer. She lifted the great house key from her side, and threatened to strike him down with it, calling aloud on Mar and Whelk and Plout, the menservants under her, to come and help her. Ere one of them could answer, however, she gave a great shriek and turned and fled, leaving the door wide open.

Curdie looked behind him, and saw an animal whose gruesome oddity even he, who knew so many of the strange creatures, two of which were never the same, that used to live inside the mountain with their masters the goblins, had never seen equalled. Its eyes were flaming with anger, but it seemed to be at the housekeeper, for it came cowering and creeping up and laid its head on the ground at Curdie's feet. Curdie hardly waited to look at it, however, but ran into the house, eager to get up the stairs before any of the men should come to annoy – he had no fear of their preventing him. Without halt or hindrance, though the passages were nearly dark, he reached the door of the princess's workroom, and knocked.

'Come in,' said the voice of the princess.

Curdie opened the door – but, to his astonishment, saw no room there. Could he have opened a wrong door? There was

the great sky, and the stars, and beneath he could see nothing—
only darkness! But what was that in the sky, straight in front
of him? A great wheel of fire, turning and turning, and
flashing out blue lights!

'Come in, Curdie,' said the voice again.

'I would at once, ma'am,' said Curdie, 'if I were sure I was
standing at your door.'

'Why should you doubt it, Curdie?'

'Because I see neither walls nor floor, only darkness and the
great sky.'

'That is all right, Curdie. Come in.'

Curdie stepped forward at once. He was indeed, for
the very crumb of a moment, tempted to feel before him
with his foot; but he saw that would be to distrust the
princess, and a greater rudeness he could not offer her. So
he stepped straight in — I will not say without a little tremble
at the thought of finding no floor beneath his foot. But
that which had need of the floor found it, and his foot was
satisfied.

No sooner was he in than he saw that the great revolving
wheel in the sky was the princess's spinning wheel, near the
other end of the room, turning very fast. He could see no sky
or stars any more, but the wheel was flashing out blue — oh,
such lovely sky-blue light! — and behind it of course sat the
princess, but whether an old woman as thin as a skeleton leaf,
or a glorious lady as young as perfection, he could not tell for
the turning and flashing of the wheel.

'Listen to the wheel,' said the voice which had already
grown dear to Curdie: its very tone precious like a jewel, not
as a jewel, for no jewel could compare with it in precious-
ness.

And Curdie listened and listened.

'What is it saying?' asked the voice.

'It is singing,' answered Curdie.

'What is it singing?'

Curdie tried to make out, but thought he could not; for no sooner had he got hold of something than it vanished again. Yet he listened, and listened, entranced with delight.

'Thank you, Curdie,' said the voice.

'Ma'am,' said Curdie, 'I did try hard for a while, but I could not make anything of it.'

'Oh yes, you did, and you have been telling it to me! Shall I tell you again what I told my wheel, and my wheel told you, and you have just told me without knowing it?'

'Please, ma'am.'

Then the lady began to sing, and her wheel spun an accompaniment to her song, and the music of the wheel was like the music of an Aeolian harp blown upon by the wind that bloweth where it listeth. Oh, the sweet sounds of that spinning wheel! Now they were gold, now silver, now grass, now palm trees, now ancient cities, now rubies, now mountain brooks, now peacock's feathers, now clouds, now snowdrops, and now mid-sea islands. But for the voice that sang through it all, about that I have no words to tell. It would make you weep if I were able to tell you what that was like, it was so beautiful and true and lovely. But this is something like the words of its song:

> The stars are spinning their threads,
>   And the clouds are the dust that flies,
> And the suns are weaving them up
>   For the time when the sleepers shall rise.

The ocean in music rolls,
    And gems are turning to eyes,
And the trees are gathering souls
    For the day when the sleepers shall rise.

The weepers are learning to smile.
    And laughter to glean the sighs;
Burn and bury the care and guile,
    For the day when the sleepers shall rise.

Oh, the dews and the moths and the daisy red,
    The larks and the glimmers and flows!
The lilies and sparrows and daily bread,
    And the something that nobody knows!

The princess stopped, her wheel stopped, and she laughed. And her laugh was sweeter than song and wheel; sweeter than running brook and silver bell; sweeter than joy itself, for the heart of the laugh was love.

'Come now, Curdie, to this side of my wheel, and you will find me,' she said; and her laugh seemed sounding on still in the words, as if they were made of breath that had laughed.

Curdie obeyed, and passed the wheel, and there she stood to receive him! — fairer than when he saw her last, a little younger still, and dressed not in green and emeralds, but in pale blue, with a coronet of silver set with pearls, and slippers covered with opals that gleamed every colour of the rainbow. It was some time before Curdie could take his eyes from the marvel of her loveliness. Fearing at last that he was rude, he turned them away; and, behold, he was in a room that was for beauty marvellous! The lofty ceiling was all a golden vine, whose great clusters of carbuncles, rubies, and chrysoberyls hung down like the bosses of groined arches, and in its centre hung the most glorious lamp that human eyes ever saw — the Silver Moon itself, a globe of silver, as it seemed, with a heart of light so wondrous potent that it rendered the mass translucent, and altogether radiant.

The room was so large that, looking back, he could scarcely see the end at which he entered; but the other was only a few yards from him — and there he saw another wonder: on a huge hearth a great fire was burning, and the fire was a huge heap of roses, and yet it was fire. The smell of the roses filled the air, and the heat of the flames of them glowed upon his face. He turned an inquiring look upon the lady, and saw that she was now seated in an ancient chair, the legs of which were crusted with gems, but the upper part like a nest of daisies and moss and green grass.

'Curdie,' she said in answer to his eyes, 'you have stood more than one trial already, and have stood them well: now I am going to put you to a harder. Do you think you are prepared for it?'

'How can I tell, ma'am,' he returned, 'seeing I do not know what it is, or what preparation it needs? Judge me yourself, ma'am.'

'It needs only trust and obedience,' answered the lady.

'I dare not say anything, ma'am. If you think me fit, command me.'

'It will hurt you terribly, Curdie, but that will be all; no real hurt but much good will come to you from it.'

Curdie made no answer but stood gazing with parted lips in the lady's face.

'Go and thrust both your hands into that fire,' she said

quickly, almost hurriedly.

Curdie dared not stop to think. It was much too terrible to think about. He rushed to the fire, and thrust both of his hands right into the middle of the heap of flaming roses, and his arms halfway up to the elbows. And it *did* hurt! But he did not draw them back. He held the pain as if it were a thing that would kill him if he let it go — as indeed it would have done. He was in terrible fear lest it should conquer him.

But when it had risen to the pitch that he thought he *could* bear it no longer, it began to fall again, and went on growing less and less until by contrast with its former severity it had become rather pleasant. At last it ceased altogether, and Curdie thought his hands must be burned to cinders if not ashes, for he did not feel them at all. The princess told him to take them out and look at them. He did so, and found that all that was gone of them was the rough, hard skin; they were white and smooth like the princess's.

'Come to me,' she said.

He obeyed and saw, to his surprise, that her face looked as if she had been weeping.

'Oh, Princess! What *is* the matter?' he cried. 'Did I make a noise and vex you?'

'No, Curdie,' she answered; 'but it was very bad.'

'Did you feel it too then?'

'Of course I did. But now it is over, and all is well. Would you like to know why I made you put your hands in the fire?'

Curdie looked at them again — then said:

'To take the marks of the work off them and make them fit for the king's court, I suppose.'

'No, Curdie,' answered the princess, shaking her head, for she was not pleased with the answer. 'It would be a poor way

63

of making your hands fit for the king's court to take off them signs of his service. There is a far greater difference on them than that. Do you feel none?'

'No, ma'am.'

'You will, though, by and by, when the time comes. But perhaps even then you might not know what had been given you, therefore I will tell you. Have you ever heard what some philosophers say — that men were all animals once?'

'No, ma'am.'

'It is of no consequence. But there is another thing that is of the greatest consequence — this: that all men, if they do not take care, go down hill to the animals' country; that many men are actually, all their lives, going to be beasts. People knew it once, but it is long since they forgot it.'

'I am not surprised to hear it, ma'am, when I think of some of our miners.'

'Ah! But you must beware, Curdie, how you say of this man or that man that he is travelling beastward. There are not nearly so many going that way as at first sight you might think. When you met your father on the hill tonight, you stood and spoke together on the same spot; and although one of you was going up and the other coming down, at a little distance no one could have told which was bound in the one direction and which in the other. Just so two people may be at the same spot in manners and behaviour, and yet one may be getting better and the other worse, which is just the greatest of all differences that could possibly exist between them.'

'But ma'am,' said Curdie, 'where is the good of knowing that there is such a difference, if you can never know where it is?'

'Now, Curdie, you must mind exactly what words I use,

because although the right words cannot do exactly what I want them to do, the wrong words will certainly do what I do not want them to do. I did not say *you can never know*. When there is a necessity for your knowing, when you have to do important business with this or that man, there is always a way of knowing enough to keep you from any great blunder. And as you will have important business to do by and by, and that with people of whom you yet know nothing, it will be necessary that you should have some better means than usual of learning the nature of them.

'Now listen. Since it is always what they *do*, whether in their minds or their bodies, that makes men go down to be less than men, that is, beasts, the change always comes first in their hands — and first of all in the inside hands, to which the outside ones are but as the gloves. They do not know it of course; for a beast does not know that he is a beast, and the nearer a man gets to being a beast the less he knows it. Neither can their best friends, or their worst enemies indeed, *see* any difference in their hands, for they see only the living gloves of them. But there are not a few who feel a vague something repulsive in the hand of a man who is growing a beast.

'Now here is what the rosefire has done for you; it has made your hands so knowing and wise, it has brought your real hands so near the outside of your flesh gloves that you will henceforth be able to know at once the hand of a man who is growing into a beast; nay, more — you will at once feel the foot of the beast he is growing, just as if there were no glove made like a man's hand between you and it.

'Hence of course it follows that you will be able often, and with further education in zoology, will be able always to tell, not only when a man is growing a beast, but what beast he is growing to, for you will know the foot – what it is and what beast's it is. According, then, to your knowledge of that beast will be your knowledge of the man you have to do with. Only there is one beautiful and awful thing about it, that if any one gifted with this perception once uses it for his own ends, it is taken from him, and then, not knowing that it is gone, he is in a far worse condition than before, for he trusts to what he has not got.'

'How dreadful!' said Curdie. 'I must mind what I am about.'

'Yes, indeed, Curdie.'

'But may not one sometimes make a mistake without being able to help it?'

'Yes. But so long as he is not after his own ends, he will never make a serious mistake.'

'I suppose you want me, ma'am, to warn every one whose hand tells me that he is growing a beast – because, as you say, he does not know it himself.'

The princess smiled.

'Much good that would do, Curdie! I don't say there are no cases in which it would be of use, but they are very rare and peculiar cases, and if such come you will know them. To such a person there is in general no insult like the truth. He cannot endure it, not because he is growing a beast, but because he is ceasing to be a man. It is the dying man in him that it makes uncomfortable, and he trots, or creeps, or swims, or flutters out of its way – calls it a foolish feeling, a whim, an old wives' fable, a bit of priests' humbug, an effete superstition, and so on.'

'And is there no hope for him? Can nothing be done? It's so awful to think of going down, down, down like that!'

'Even when it's with his own will?'

'That's what seems to me to make it worst of all,' said Curdie.

'You are right,' answered the princess, nodding her head; 'but there is this amount of excuse to make for all such, remember – that they do not know what or how horrid their coming fate is. Many a lady, so delicate and nice that she can bear nothing coarser than the finest linen to tuch her body, if she had a mirror that could show her the animal she is growing to, as it lies waiting within the fair skin and the fine linen and the silk and the jewels, would receive a shock that might possibly wake her up.'

'Why then, ma'am, shouldn't she have it?'

The princess held her peace.

'Come here, Lina,' she said after a long pause.

From somewhere behind Curdie, crept forward the same hideous animal which had fawned at his feet at the door, and which, without his knowing it, had followed him every step up the dove tower. She ran to the princess, and lay down at her feet, looking up at her with an expression so pitiful that in Curdie's heart is overcame all the ludicrousness of her horrible mass of incongruities. She had a very short body, and very long legs made like an elephant's, so that in lying down she kneeled with both pairs. her tail, which dragged on the floor behind her, was twice as long and quite as thick as her body. Her head was something between that of a polar bear and a snake. Her eyes were dark green, with a yellow light in them. Her under teeth came up like a fringe of icicles, only very white, outside of her upper lip. Her throat looked as if the hair had been plucked off. It showed a skin white and smooth.

'Give Curdie a paw, Lina,' said the princess.

The creature rose, and, lifting a long foreleg, held up a great doglike paw to Curdie. He took it gently. But what a shudder, as of terrified delight, ran through him, when, instead of the paw of a dog, such as it seemed to his eyes, he clasped in his great mining fist the soft, neat little hand of a child! He took it in both of his, and held it as if he could not let it go. The green eyes stared at him with their yellow light, and the mouth was turned up towards him with its constant half grin; but here *was* the child's hand! If he could but pull the child out of the beast! His eyes sought the princess. She was watching him with evident satisfaction.

'Ma'am, here is a child's hand!' said Curdie.

'Your gift does more for you than it promised. It is yet better to perceive a hidden good than a hidden evil.'

'But,' began Curdie.

'I am not going to answer any more questions this evening,' interrupted the princess. 'You have not half got to the bottom of the answers I have already given you. That paw in your hand now might almost teach you the whole science of natural history — the heavenly sort, I mean.'

'I will think,' said Curdie. 'But oh! please! one word more: may I tell my father and mother all about it?'

'Certainly — though perhaps now it may be their turn to find it a little difficult to believe that things went just as you must tell them.'

'They shall see that I believe it all this time,' said Curdie.

'Tell them that tomorrow morning you must set out for the court — not like a great man, but just as poor as you are. They had better not speak about it. Tell them also that it will be a long time before they hear of you again, but they must not lose heart. And tell your father to lay that stone I gave him last night in a safe place – not because of the greatness of its price, although it is such an emerald as no prince has in his crown, but because it will be a newsbearer between you and him. As often as he gets at all anxious about you, he must take it and lay it in the fire, and leave it there when he goes to bed. In the morning he must find it in the ashes, and if it be as green as ever, then all goes well with you; if it have lost colour, things go ill with you; but if it be very pale indeed, then you are in great danger, and he must come to me.'

'Yes, ma'am,' said Curdie. 'Please, am I to go now?'

'Yes,' answered the princess, and held out her hand to him.

Curdie took it, trembling with joy. It was a very beautiful hand – not small, very smooth, but not very soft – and just the same to his fire-taught touch that it was to his eyes. He would have stood there all night holding it if she had not gently withdrawn it.

'I will provide you a servant,' she said, 'for your journey, and to wait upon you afterward.'

'But where am I to go, ma'am, and what am I to do? You have given me no message to carry, neither have you said what I am wanted for. I go without a notion whether I am to walk this way or that, or what I am to do when I get I don't know where.'

'Curdie!' said the princess, and there was a tone of reminder in his own name as she spoke it, 'did I not tell you to tell your father and mother that you were to set out for the court? And you *know* that lies to the north. You must learn to use far less direct directions than that. You must not be like a dull servant that needs to be told again and again before he will understand. You have orders enough to start with, and you will find, as you go on, and as you need to know, what you have to do. But I warn you that perhaps it will not look the least like what you may have been fancying I should require of you. I have one idea of you and your work, and you have another. I do not blame you for that — you cannot help it yet; but you must be ready to let my idea, which sets you working, set your idea right. Be true and honest and fearless, and all shall go well with you and your work, and all with whom your work lies, and so with your parents — and me too, Curdie,' she added after a little pause.

The young miner bowed his head low, patted the strange head that lay at the princess's feet, and turned away.

As soon as he passed the spinning wheel, which looked, in the midst of the glorious room, just like any wheel you might find in a country cottage — old and worn and dingy and dusty — the splendour of the place vanished, and he saw but the big bare room he seemed at first to have entered, with the moon — the princess's moon no doubt — shining in at one of the windows upon the spinning wheel.

CHAPTER NINE

Hands

CURDIE went home, pondering much, and told everything to his father and mother. As the old princess had said, it was now their turn to find what they heard hard to believe. If they had not been able to trust Curdie himself, they would have refused to believe more than the half of what he reported, then they would have refused that half too, and at last would most likely for a time have disbelieved in the very existence of the princess, what evidence their own senses had given them notwithstanding.

For he had nothing conclusive to show in proof of what he told them. When he held out his hands to them, his mother said they looked as if he had been washing them with soft soap, only they did smell of something nicer than that, and she must allow it was more like roses than anything else she knew. His father could not see any difference upon his hands, but then it was night, he said, and their poor little lamp was not enough for his old eyes. As to the feel of them, each of his own hands, he said, was hard and horny enough for two, and it must be the fault of the dullness of his own thick skin that he felt no change on Curdie's palms.

'Here, Curdie,' said his mother, 'try my hand, and see what

beast's paw lies inside it.'

'No, Mother,' answered Curdie, half beseeching, half indignant, 'I will not insult my new gift by making pretence to try it. That would be mockery. There is no hand within yours but the hand of a true woman, my mother.'

'I should like you just to take hold of my hand though,' said his mother. 'You are my son, and may know all the bad there is in me.'

Then at once Curdie took her hand in his. And when he had it, he kept it, stroking it gently with his other hand.

'Mother,' he said at length, 'your hand feels just like that of the princess.'

'What! My horny, cracked, rheumatic old hand, with its big joints, and its short nails all worn down to the quick with hard work – like the hand of the beautiful princess! Why, my child, you will make me fancy your fingers have grown very dull indeed, instead of sharp and delicate, if you talk such nonsense. Mine is such an ugly hand I should be ashamed to show it to any but one that loved me. But love makes all safe – doesn't it, Curdie?'

'Well, Mother, all I can say is that I don't feel a roughness, or a crack, or a big joint, or a short nail. Your hand feels just and exactly, as near as I can recollect, and it's not more than two hours since I had it in mine – well, I will say, very like indeed to that of the old princess.'

'Go away, you flatterer,' said his mother, with a smile that showed how she prized the love that lay beneath what she took for its hyperbole. The praise even which one cannot accept is sweet from a true mouth. 'If that is all your new gift can do, it won't make a warlock of you,' she added.

'Mother, it tells me nothing but the truth,' insisted Curdie, 'however unlike the truth it may seem. It wants no gift to tell what anybody's outside hands are like. But by it I *know* your inside hands are like the princess's.'

'And I am sure the boy speaks true,' said Peter. 'He only says about your hand what I have known ever so long about yourself, Joan. Curdie, your mother's foot is as pretty a foot as any lady's in the land, and where her hand is not so pretty it comes of killing its beauty for you and me, my boy. And I can tell you more, Curdie. I don't know much about ladies and gentlemen, but I am sure your inside mother must be a lady, as her hand tells you, and I will try to say how I know it. This is how: when I forget myself looking at her as she goes about her work – and that happens often as I grow older – I fancy for a moment or two that I am a gentleman; and when I wake up from my little dream, it is only to feel the more strongly that I must do everything as a gentleman should. I will try to tell you what I mean, Curdie. If a gentleman – I mean a real gentleman, not a pretended one, of which sort they say there are a many above ground – if a real gentleman were to lose all his money and come down to work in the mines to get bread for his family – do you think, Curdie, he would work like the lazy ones? Would he try to do as little as he could for his wages? I know the sort of the true gentleman – pretty near as well as he does himself. And my wife, that's your mother, Curdie, she's a true lady, you may take my word for it, for it's she that makes me want to be a true gentleman. Wife, the boy is in the right about your hand.'

'Now, Father, let me feel yours,' said Curdie, daring a little more.

'No, no, my boy,' answered Peter. 'I don't want to hear anything about my hand or my head or my heart. I am what I

73

am, and I hope growing better, and that's enough. No, you shan't feel my hand. You must go to bed, for you must start with the sun.'

It was not as if Curdie had been leaving them to go to prison, or to make a fortune, and although they were sorry enough to lose him, they were not in the least heartbroken or even troubled at his going.

As the princess had said he was to go like the poor man he was, Curdie came down in the morning from his little loft dressed in his working clothes. His mother, who was busy getting his breakfast for him, while his father sat reading to her out of an old book, would have had him put on his holiday garments, which, she said, would look poor enough among the fine ladies and gentlemen he was going to. But Curdie said he did not know that he was going among ladies and gentlemen, and that as work was better than play, his workday clothes must on the whole be better than his playday clothes; and as his father accepted the argument, his mother gave in.

When he had eaten his breakfast, she took a pouch made of goatskin, with the long hair on it, filled it with bread and cheese, and hung it over his shoulder. Then his father gave him a stick he had cut for him in the wood, and he bade them good-bye rather hurriedly, for he was afraid of breaking down. As he went out he caught up his mattock and took it with him. It had on the one side a pointed curve of strong steel for loosening the earth and the ore, and on the other a steel hammer for breaking the stones and rocks. Just as he crossed the threshold the sun showed the first segment of his disc above the horizon.

CHAPTER TEN

The Heath

HE had to go to the bottom of the hill to get into a country he could cross, for the mountains to the north were full of precipices, and it would have been losing time to go that way. Not until he had reached the king's house was it any use to turn northwards. Many a look did he raise, as he passed it, to the dove tower, and as long as it was in sight, but he saw nothing of the lady of the pigeons.

On and on he fared, and came in a few hours to a country where there were no mountains more – only hills, with great stretches of desolate heath. Here and there was a village, but that brought him little pleasure, for the people were rougher and worse mannered than those in the mountains, and as he passed through, the children came behind and mocked him.

'There's a monkey running away from the mines!' they cried.

Sometimes their parents came out and encouraged them.

'He doesn't want to find gold for the king any longer – the lazybones!' they would say. 'He'll be well taxed down here though, and he won't like that either.'

But it was little to Curdie that men who did not know what he was about should not approve of his proceedings. He gave them a merry answer now and then, and held diligently on his way. When they got so rude as nearly to make him angry, he would treat them as he used to treat the goblins, and sing his own songs to keep out their foolish noises. Once a child fell as he turned to run away after throwing a stone at him. He picked him up, kissed him, and carried him to his mother. The woman had run out in terror when she saw the strange miner about, as she thought, to take vengeance on her boy. When he put him in her arms, she blessed him, and Curdie went on his way rejoicing.

And so the day went on, and the evening came, and in the middle of a great desolate heath he began to feel tired, and sat down under an ancient hawthorn, through which every now and then a lone wind that seemed to come from nowhere and to go nowhither sighed and hissed. It was very old and distorted. There was not another tree for miles all round. It seemed to have lived so long, and to have been so torn and tossed by the tempests on that moor, that it had at last gathered a wind of its own, which got up now and then, tumbled itself about, and lay down again.

Curdie had been so eager to get on that he had eaten nothing since his breakfast. But he had had plenty of water, for many little streams had crossed his path. He now opened the wallet his mother had given him, and began to eat his supper. The sun was setting. A few clouds had gathered about the west, but there was not a single cloud anywhere else to be seen.

Now Curdie did not know that this was a part of the country very hard to get through. Nobody lived there, though many had tried to build in it. Some died very soon. Some rushed out of it. Those who stayed longest went raving mad, and died a terrible death. Such as walked straight on, and did not spend a night there, got through well and were nothing the worse. But those who slept even a single night in it were sure to meet with something they could never forget, and which often left a mark everybody could read. And that old hawthorn might have been enough for a warning – it looked so like a human being dried up and distorted with age and suffering, with cares instead of loves, and things instead of thoughts. Both it and the heath around it, which stretched on all sides as far as he could see, were so withered that it was impossible to say whether they were alive or not.

And while Curdie ate there came a change. Clouds had gathered over his head, and seemed drifting about in every direction, as if not 'shepherded by the slow, unwilling wind,' but hunted in all directions by wolfish flaws across the plains of the sky. The sun was going down in a storm of lurid crimson, and out of the west came a wind that felt red and hot the one moment, and cold and pale the other. And very strangely it sang in the dreary old hawthorn tree, and very cheerily it blew about Curdie, now making him creep close up to the tree for shelter from its shivery cold, now fan himself with his cap, it was so sultry and stifling. It seemed to come from the deathbed of the sun, dying in fever and ague.

And as he gazed at the sun, now on the verge of the horizon, very large and very red and very dull – for though the clouds had broken away a dusty fog was spread all over the disc – Curdie saw something strange appear against it, moving about like a fly over its burning face. This looked as if it were coming out of the sun's furnace heart, and was a living creature of some kind surely; but its shape was very uncertain, because the dazzle of the light all around melted the outlines.

77

It was growing larger, it must be approaching! It grew so rapidly that by the time the sun was half down its head reached the top of the arch, and presently nothing but its legs were to be seen, crossing and recrossing the face of the vanishing disc.

When the sun was down he could see nothing of it more, but in a moment he heard its feet galloping over the dry crackling heather, and seeming to come straight for him. He stood up, lifted his pickaxe, and threw the hammer end over his shoulder: he was going to have a fight for his life! And now it appeared again, vague, yet very awful, in the dim twilight the sun had left behind. But just before it reached him, down from its four long legs it dropped flat on the ground, and came crawling towards him, wagging a huge tail as it came.

CHAPTER ELEVEN

Lina

IT was Lina. All at once Curdie recognized her – the frightful creature he had seen at the princess's. He dropped his pickaxe, and held out his hand. She crept nearer and nearer, and laid her chin in his palm, and he patted her ugly head. Then she crept away behind the tree, and lay down, panting hard. Curdie did not much like the idea of her being behind him. Horrible as she was to look at, she seemed to his mind more horrible when he was not looking at her. But he remembered the child's hand, and never thought of driving her away. Now and then he gave a glance behind him, and there she lay flat, with her eyes closed and her terrible teeth gleaming between her two huge forepaws.

After his supper and his long day's journey it was no wonder Curdie should now be sleepy. Since the sun set the air had been warm and pleasant. He lay down under the tree, closed his eyes, and thought to sleep. He found himself mistaken, however. But although he could not sleep, he was yet aware of resting delightfully.

Presently he heard a sweet sound of singing somewhere, such as he had never heard before – a singing as of curious birds far off, which drew nearer and nearer. At length he heard their wings, and, opening his eyes, saw a number of very large birds, as it seemed, alighting around him, still singing. It was strange to hear song from the throats of such big birds.

And still singing, with large and round but not the less birdlike voices, they began to weave a strange dance about him, moving their wings in time with their legs. But the dance seemed somehow to be troubled and broken, and to return upon itself in an eddy, in place of sweeping smoothly on. And he soon learned, in the low short growls behind him, the cause of the imperfection: they wanted to dance all round the tree, but Lina would not permit them to come on her side.

Now Curdie liked the birds, and did not altogether *like* Lina. But neither, nor both together, made a *reason* for driving away the princess's creature. Doubtless she *had been* the goblins' creature, but the last time he saw her was in the king's house and the dove tower, and at the old princess's feet. So he left her to do as she would, and the dance of the birds continued only a semicircle, troubled at the edges, and returning upon itself.

But their song and their motions, nevertheless, and the waving of their wings, began at length to make him very sleepy. All the time he had kept doubting whether they could really be birds, and the sleepier he got, the more he imagined them something else, but he suspected no harm.

Suddenly, just as he was sinking beneath the waves of slumber, he awoke in fierce pain. The birds were upon him — all over him — and had begun to tear him with beaks and claws. He had but time, however, to feel that he could not move under their weight, when they set up a hideous screaming, and scattered like a cloud. Lina was among them, snapping and striking with her paws, while her tail knocked them over and over. But they flew up, gathered, and descended on her in a swarm, perching upon every part of her body, so that he could see only a huge misshapen mass, which seemed to go rolling away into the darkness. He got up and tried to follow, but could see nothing, and after wandering about hither and thither for some time, found himself again beside the hawthorn.

He feared greatly that the birds had been too much for Lina, and had torn her to pieces. In a little while, however, she came limping back, and lay down in her old place. Curdie also lay down, but, from the pain of his wounds, there was no sleep for him. When the light came he found his clothes a good deal torn and his skin as well, but gladly wondered why the wicked birds had not at once attacked his eyes. Then he turned looking for Lina. She rose and crept to him. But she was in far worse plight than he – plucked and gashed and torn with the beaks and claws of the birds, especially about the bare part of her neck, so that she was pitiful to see. And those worst wounds she could not reach to lick.

'Poor Lina!' said Curdie, 'you got all those helping me.'

She wagged her tail, and made it clear she understood him. Then it flashed upon Curdie's mind that perhaps this was the companion the princess had promised him. For the princess did so many things differently from what anybody looked for! Lina was no beauty certainly, but already, the first night, she had saved his life.

'Come along, Lina,' he said, 'we want water.'

She put her nose to the earth, and after snuffing for a moment, darted off in a straight line. Curdie followed. The ground was so uneven, that after losing sight of her many times, at last he seemed to have lost her altogether. In a few minutes, however, he came upon her waiting for him. Instantly she darted off again. After he had lost and found her again many times, he found her the last time lying beside a great stone. As soon as he came up she began scratching at it with her paws. When he had raised it an inch or two, she shoved in first her nose and then her teeth, and lifted with all the might of her neck.

When at length between them they got it up, there was a beautiful little well. He filled his cap with the clearest and sweetest water, and drank. Then he gave to Lina, and she drank plentifully. Next he washed her wounds very carefully. And as he did so, he noted how much the bareness of her neck added to the strange repulsiveness of her appearance. Then he bethought him of the goatskin wallet his mother had given him, and taking it from his shoulders, tried whether it would do to make a collar of for the poor animal. He found there was just enough, and the hair so similar in colour to Lina's that no one could suspect it of having grown somewhere else.

He took his knife, ripped up the seams of the wallet, and began tying the skin to her neck. It was plain she understood perfectly what he wished, for she endeavoured to hold her neck conveniently, turning it this way and that while he contrived, with his rather scanty material, to make the collar fit. As his mother had taken care to provide him with needles and thread, he soon had a nice gorget ready for her. He laced it on with one of his boot laces, which its long hair covered. Poor Lina looked much better in it. Nor could any one have called it a piece of finery. If ever green eyes with a yellow light in them looked grateful, hers did.

As they had no longer any bag to carry them in, Curdie and

Lina now ate what was left of the provisions. Then they set out again upon their journey. For seven days it lasted. They met with various adventures, and in all of them Lina proved so helpful, and so ready to risk her life for the sake of her companion, that Curdie grew not merely very fond but very trustful of her; and her ugliness, which at first only moved his pity, now actually increased his affection for her. One day, looking at her stretched on the grass before him, he said:

'Oh, Lina! If the princess would but burn you in her fire of roses!'

She looked up at him, gave a mournful whine like a dog, and laid her head on his feet. What or how much he could not tell, but clearly she had gathered something from his words.

CHAPTER TWELVE

More Creatures

ONE day from morning till night they had been passing through a forest. As soon as the sun was down Curdie began to be aware that there were more in it than themselves. First he saw only the swift rush of a figure across the trees at some distance. Then he saw another and then another at shorter intervals. Then he saw others both farther off and nearer. At last, missing Lina and looking about after her, he saw an appearance as marvellous as herself steal up to her, and begin conversing with her after some beast fashion which evidently she understood.

Presently what seemed a quarrel arose between them, and stranger noises followed, mingled with growling. At length it came to a fight, which had not lasted long, however, before the creature of the wood threw itself upon its back, and held up its paws to Lina. She instantly walked on, and the creature got up and followed her. They had not gone far before another strange animal appeared, approaching Lina, when precisely the same thing was repeated, the vanquished animal rising and following with the former. Again, and yet again, and again, a fresh animal came up, seemed to be reasoned and certainly was fought with and overcome by Lina, until at last, before they were out of the wood, she was followed by forty-nine of the most grotesquely ugly, the most extravagantly abnormal animals imagination can conceive. To describe them were a hopeless task.

I knew a boy who used to make animals out of heather roots. Wherever he could find four legs, he was pretty sure to find a head and a tail. His beasts were a most comic menagerie, and right fruitful of laughter. But they were not so grotesque and extravagant as Lina and her followers. One of them, for instance, was like a boa constrictor walking on four little stumpy legs near its tail. About the same distance from its head were two little wings, which it was forever fluttering as if trying to fly with them. Curdie thought it fancied it did fly with them, when it was merely plodding on busily with its four little stumps. How it managed to keep up he could not think, till once when he missed it from the group: the same moment he caught sight of something at a distance plunging at an awful serpentine rate through the trees, and presently, from behind a huge ash, this same creature fell again into the group, quietly waddling along on its four stumps.

Watching it after this, he saw that, when it was not able to keep up any longer, and they had all got a little space ahead, it shot into the wood away from the route, and made a great round, serpenting along in huge billows of motion, devouring the ground, undulating awfully, galloping as if it were all legs together, and its four stumps nowhere. In this mad fashion it shot ahead, and, a few minutes after, toddled in again among the rest, walking peacefully and somewhat painfully on its few fours.

From the time it takes to describe one of them it will be readily seen that it would hardly do to attempt a description of each of the forty-nine. They were not a goodly company, but well worth contemplating, nevertheless; and Curdie had been too long used to the goblins' creatures in the mines and on the mountain, to feel the least uncomfortable at being followed by such a herd. On the contrary, the marvellous vagaries of shape they manifested amused him greatly, and shortened the journey much.

Before they were all gathered, however, it had got so dark that he could see some of them only a part at a time, and every now and then, as the company wandered on, he would be startled by some extraordinary limb or feature, undreamed of by him before, thrusting itself out of the darkness into the range of his ken. Probably there were some of his old acquaintances among them, although such had been the conditions of semi-darkness, in which alone he had ever seen any of them, that it was not like he would be able to identify any of them.

On they marched solemnly, almost in silence, for either with feet or voice the creatures seldom made any noise. By the time they reached the outside of the wood it was morning twilight. Into the open trooped the strange torrent of deformity, each one following Lina. Suddenly she stopped, turned towards them, and said something which they understood, although to Curdie's ear the sounds she made seemed to have no articulation. Instantly they all turned, and vanished in the forest, and Lina alone came trotting lithely and clumsily after her master.

CHAPTER THIRTEEN

The Baker's Wife

THEY were now passing through a lovely country of hill and dale and rushing stream. The hills were abrupt, with broken chasms for watercourses, and deep little valleys full of trees. But now and then they came to a larger valley, with a fine river, whose level banks and the adjacent meadows were dotted all over with red and white kine, while on the fields above, that sloped a little to the foot of the hills, grew oats and barley and wheat, and on the sides of the hills themselves vines hung and chestnuts rose.

They came at last to a broad, beautiful river, up which they must go to arrive at the city of Gwyntystorm, where the king had his court. As they went the valley narrowed, and then the river, but still it was wide enough for large boats. After this, while the river kept its size, the banks narrowed, until there was only room for a road between the river and the great cliffs that overhung it. At last river and road took a sudden turn, and lo! a great rock in the river, which dividing flowed around it, and on the top of the rock the city, with lofty walls and towers and battlements, and above the city the palace of the king, built like a strong castle. But the fortifications had long been neglected, for the whole country was now under one king, and all men said there was no more need for weapons or walls. No man pretended to love his neighbour, but every one said he knew that peace and quiet behaviour was the best thing for himself, and that, he said, was quite as useful, and a great deal more reasonable. The city was prosperous and rich, and if everybody was not comfortable, everybody else said he ought to be.

When Curdie got up opposite the mighty rock, which sparkled all over with crystals, he found a narrow bridge, defended by gates and portcullis and towers with loopholes. But the gates stood wide open, and were dropping from their great hinges; the portcullis was eaten away with rust, and clung to the grooves evidently immovable; while the loopholed towers had neither floor nor roof, and their tops were fast filling up their interiors. Curdie thought it a pity, if only for their old story, that they should be thus neglected. But everybody in the city regarded these signs of decay as the best proof of the prosperity of the place. Commerce and self-interest, they said, had got the better of violence, and the troubles of the past were whelmed in the riches that flowed in at their open gates.

Indeed, there was one sect of philosophers in it which taught that it would be better to forget all the past history of the city, were it not that its former imperfections taught its present inhabitants how superior they and their times were, and enabled them to glory over their ancestors. There were even certain quacks in the city who advertised pills for enabling people to think well of themselves, and some few bought of them, but most laughed, and said, with evident truth, that they did not require them. Indeed, the general theme of discourse when they met was, how much wiser they were than their fathers.

Curdie crossed the river, and began to ascend the winding road that led up to the city. They met a good many idlers, and all stared at them. It was no wonder they should stare, but there was an unfriendliness in their looks which Curdie did not like. No one, however, offered them any molestation: Lina did not invite liberties. After a long ascent, they reached the principal gate of the city and entered.

The street was very steep, ascending toward the palace, which rose in great strength above all the houses. Just as they entered, a baker, whose shop was a few doors inside the gate, came out in his white apron, and ran to the shop of his friend, the barber, on the opposite side of the way. But as he ran he stumbled and fell heavily. Curdie hastened to help him up, and found he had bruised his forehead badly. He swore grievously at the stone for tripping him up, declaring it was the third time he had fallen over it within the last month; and saying what was the king about that he allowed such a stone to stick up forever on the main street of his royal residence of Gwyntystorm! What was a king for if he would not take care of his people's heads! And he stroked his forehead tenderly.

'Was it your head or your feet that ought to bear the blame of your fall?' asked Curdie.

'Why, you booby of a miner! My feet, of course,' answered the baker.

'Nay, then,' said Curdie, 'the king can't be to blame.'

'Oh, I see!' said the baker. 'You're laying a trap for me. Of course, if you come to that, it was my head that ought to have looked after my feet. But it is the king's part to look after us all, and have his streets smooth.'

'Well, I don't see,' said Curdie, 'why the king should take

care of the baker, when the baker's head won't take care of the baker's feet.'

'Who are you to make game of the king's baker?' cried the man in a rage.

But, instead of answering, Curdie went up to the bump on the street which had repeated itself on the baker's head, and turning the hammer end of his mattock, struck it such a blow that it flew wide in pieces. Blow after blow he struck until he had levelled it with the street.

But out flew the barber upon him in a rage.

'What do you break my window for, you rascal, with your pickaxe?'

'I am very sorry,' said Curdie. 'It must have been a bit of stone that flew from my mattock. I couldn't help it, you know.'

'Couldn't help it! A fine story! What do you go breaking the rock for — the very rock upon which the city stands?'

'Look at your friend's forehead,' said Curdie. 'See what a lump he has got on it with falling over that same stone.'

'What's that to my window?' cried the barber. 'His forehead can mend itself; my poor window can't.'

'But he's the king's baker,' said Curdie, more and more surprised at the man's anger.

'What's that to me? This is a free city. Every man here takes care of himself, and the king takes care of us all. I'll have the price of my window out of you, or the exchequer shall pay for it.'

Something caught Curdie's eye. He stooped, picked up a piece of the stone he had just broken, and put it in his pocket.

'I suppose you are going to break another of my windows with that stone!' said the barber.

'Oh no,' said Curdie. 'I didn't mean to break your window, and I certainly won't break another.'

'Give me that stone,' said the barber.

Curdie gave it him, and the barber threw it over the city wall.

'I thought you wanted the stone,' said Curdie.

'No, you fool!' answered the barber. 'What should I want with a stone?'

Curdie stooped and picked up another.

'Give me that stone,' said the barber.

'No,' answered Curdie. 'You have just told me you don't want a stone, and I do.'

The barber took Curdie by the collar.

'Come, now! You pay me for that window.'

'How much?' asked Curdie.

The barber said, 'A crown.' But the baker, annoyed at the heartlessness of the barber, in thinking more of his broken window than the bump on his friend's forehead, interfered.

'No, no,' he said to Curdie; 'don't you pay any such sum. A little pane like that cost only a quarter.'

'Well, to be certain,' said Curdie, 'I'll give a half.' For he doubted the baker as well as the barber. 'Perhaps one day, if he finds he has asked too much, he will bring me the difference.'

'Ha! ha!' laughed the barber. 'A fool and his money are soon parted.'

But as he took the coin from Curdie's hand he grasped it in affected reconciliation and real satisfaction. In Curdie's, his was the cold smooth leathery palm of a monkey. He looked up, almost expecting to see him pop the money in his cheek; but he had not yet got so far as that, though he was well on the road to it: then he would have no other pocket.

'I'm glad that stone is gone, anyhow,' said the baker. 'It was the bane of my life. I had no idea how easy it was to remove it. Give me your pickaxe, young miner, and I will show you how a baker can make the stones fly.'

He caught the tool out of Curdie's hand, and flew at one of the foundation stones of the gateway. But he jarred his arm terribly, scarcely chipped the stone, dropped the mattock with a cry of pain, and ran into his own shop. Curdie picked up his implement, and, looking after the baker, saw bread in the window, and followed him in. But the baker, ashamed of himself, and thinking he was coming to laugh at him, popped out of the back door, and when Curdie entered, the baker's wife came from the bakehouse to serve him. Curdie requested to know the price of a certain good-sized loaf.

Now the baker's wife had been watching what had passed since first her husband ran out of the shop, and she liked the look of Curdie. Also she was more honest than her husband. Casting a glance to the back door, she replied:

'That is not the best bread. I will sell you a loaf of what we bake for ourselves.' And when she had spoken she laid a finger on her lips. 'Take care of yourself in this place, my son,' she added. 'They do not love strangers. I was once a stranger here, and I know what I say.' Then fancying she heard her husband, 'That is a strange animal you have,' she said, in a louder voice.

'Yes,' answered Curdie. 'She is no beauty, but she is very good, and we love each other. Don't we, Lina?'

Lina looked up and whined. Curdie threw her the half of his loaf, which she ate, while her master and the baker's wife talked a little. Then the baker's wife gave them some water, and Curdie having paid for his loaf, he and Lina went up the street together.

CHAPTER FOURTEEN

The Dogs of Gwyntystorm

THE steep street led them straight up to a large market place with butchers' shops, about which were many dogs. The moment they caught sight of Lina, one and all they came rushing down upon her, giving her no chance of explaining herself. When Curdie saw the dogs coming he heaved up his mattock over his shoulder, and was ready, if they would have it so. Seeing him thus prepared to defend his follower, a great ugly bulldog flew at him. With the first blow Curdie struck him through the brain and the brute fell dead at his feet. But he could not at once recover his weapon, which stuck in the skull of his foe, and a huge mastiff, seeing him thus hampered, flew at him next.

Now Lina, who had shown herself so brave upon the road thither, had grown shy upon entering the city, and kept always at Curdie's heel. But it was her turn now. The moment she saw her master in danger she seemed to go mad with rage. As the mastiff jumped at Curdie's throat, Lina flew at him, seized him with her tremendous jaws, gave one roaring grind, and he lay beside the bulldog with his neck broken. They were the best dogs in the market, after the judgement of the butchers of Gwyntystorm. Down came their masters, knives

93

in hand.

Curdie drew himself up fearlessly, mattock on shoulder, and awaited their coming, while at his heel his awful attendant showed not only her outside fringe of icicle teeth, but a double row of right serviceable fangs she wore inside her mouth, and her green eyes flashed yellow as gold. The butchers, not liking the look of either of them or of the dogs at their feet, drew back, and began to remonstrate in the manner of outraged men.

'Stranger,' said the first, 'that bulldog is mine.'

'Take him, then,' said Curdie, indignant.

'You've killed him!'

'Yes — else he would have killed me.'

'That's no business of mine.'

'No?'

'No.'

'That makes it the more mine, then.'

'This sort of thing won't do, you know,' said the other butcher.

'That's true,' said Curdie.

'That's my mastiff,' said the butcher.

'And as he ought to be,' said Curdie.

'Your brute shall be burned alive for it,' said the butcher.

'Not yet,' answered Curdie. 'We have done no wrong. We were walking quietly up your street when your dogs flew at us. If you don't teach your dogs how to treat strangers, you must take the consequences.'

'They treat them quite properly,' said the butcher. 'What right has any one to bring an abomination like that into our city? The horror is enough to make an idiot of every child in the place.'

'We are both subjects of the king, and my poor animal can't help her looks. How would you like to be served like that because you were ugly? She's not a bit fonder of her looks than you are — only what can she do to change them?'

'I'll do to change them,' said the fellow.

Thereupon the butchers brandished their long knives and advanced, keeping their eyes upon Lina.

'Don't be afraid, Lina,' cried Curdie. 'I'll kill one — you kill the other.'

Lina gave a howl that might have terrified an army, and crouched ready to spring. The butchers turned and ran.

By this time a great crowd had gathered behind the butchers, and in it a number of boys returning from school who began to stone the strangers. It was a way they had with man or beast they did not expect to make anything by. One of the stones struck Lina; she caught it in her teeth and crunched it so that it fell in gravel from her mouth. Some of the foremost of the crowd saw this, and it terrified them. They drew back; the rest took fright from their retreat; the panic spread; and at last the crowd scattered in all directions. They ran, and cried out, and said the devil and his dam were come to Gwyntystorm. So Curdie and Lina were left standing unmolested in the market place. But the terror of them spread throughout the city, and everybody began to shut and lock his door so that by the time the setting sun shone down the street, there was not a shop left open, for fear of the devil and his horrible dam. But all the upper windows within sight of them were crowded with heads watching them where they stood lonely in the deserted market place.

Curdie looked carefully all round, but could not see one open door. He caught sight of the sign of an inn, however, and laying down his mattock, and telling Lina to take care of it, walked up to the door of it and knocked. But the people in the house, instead of opening the door, threw things at him from the windows. They would not listen to a word he said, but sent him back to Lina with the blood running down his face. When Lina saw that she leaped up in a fury and was rushing at the house, into which she would certainly have broken; but Curdie called her, and made her lie down beside him while he bethought him what next he should do.

'Lina,' he said, 'the people keep their gates open, but their houses and their hearts shut.'

As if she knew it was her presence that had brought this trouble upon him, she rose and went round and round him, purring like a tigress, and rubbing herself against his legs.

Now there was one little thatched house that stood squeezed in between two tall gables, and the sides of the two great houses shot out projecting windows that nearly met across the roof of the little one, so that it lay in the street like a doll's house. In this house lived a poor woman, with a grand-child. And because she never gossiped or quarrelled, or chaffered in the market, but went without what she could not afford, the people called her a witch, and would have done her many an ill turn if they had not been afraid of her.

Now while Curdie was looking in another direction the door opened, and out came a little dark-haired, black-eyed, gypsy-looking child, and toddled across the market place toward the outcasts. The moment they saw her coming, Lina lay down flat on the road, and with her two huge forepaws covered her mouth, while Curdie went to meet her, holding out his arms. The little one came straight to him, and held up her mouth to be kissed. Then she took him by the hand, and drew him toward the house, and Curdie yielded to the silent invitation.

But when Lina rose to follow, the child shrank from her, frightened a little. Curdie took her up, and holding her on one arm, patted Lina with the other hand. Then the child wanted also to pat doggy, as she called her by a right bountiful stretch of courtesy, and having once patted her, nothing would serve but Curdie must let her have a ride on doggy. So he set her on Lina's back, holding her hand, and she rode home in merry triumph, all unconscious of the hundreds of eyes staring at her foolhardiness from the windows about the market place, or the murmur of deep disapproval that rose from as many lips.

At the door stood the grandmother to receive them. She caught the child to her bosom with delight at her courage, welcomed Curdie, and showed no dread of Lina. Many were the significant nods exchanged, and many a one said to another that the devil and the witch were old friends. But the woman was only a wise woman, who, having seen how Curdie and Lina behaved to each other, judged from that what sort they were, and so made them welcome to her house. She was not like her fellow townspeople, for that they were strangers recommended them to her.

The moment her door was shut the other doors began to open, and soon there appeared little groups here and there about a threshold, while a few of the more courageous ventured out upon the square — all ready to make for their houses again, however, upon the least sign of movement in the little thatched one.

The baker and the barber had joined one of these groups, and were busily wagging their tongues against Curdie and his horrible beast.

'He can't be honest,' said the barber: 'for he paid me double the worth of the pane he broke in my window.'

And then he told them how Curdie broke his window by breaking a stone in the street with his hammer. There the baker struck in.

'Now that was the stone,' said he, 'over which I had fallen three times within the last month: could it be by fair means he broke that to pieces at the first blow? Just to make up my mind on that point I tried his own hammer against a stone in the gate; it nearly broke both my arms, and loosened half the teeth in my head!'

CHAPTER FIFTEEN

Derba and Barbara

MEANTIME the wanderers were hospitably entertained by the old woman and her grandchild and they were all very comfortable and happy together. Little Barbara sat upon Curdie's knee, and he told her stories about the mines and his adventures in them. But he never mentioned the king or the princess, for all that story was hard to believe. And he told her about his mother and father, and how good they were. And Derba sat and listened. At last little Barbara fell asleep in Curdie's arms, and her grandmother carried her to bed.

It was a poor little house, and Derba gave up her own room to Curdie because he was honest and talked wisely. Curdie saw how it was, and begged her to allow him to lie on the floor, but she would not hear of it.

In the night he was waked by Lina pulling at him. As soon as he spoke to her she ceased, and Curdie, listening, thought he heard someone trying to get in. He rose, took his mattock, and went about the house, listening and watching; but although he heard noises now at one place now at another, he could not think what they meant for no one appeared. Certainly, considering how she had frightened them all in the day, it was not likely any one would attack Lina at night. By and by the noises ceased, and Curdie went back to his bed, and slept undisturbed.

In the morning, however, Derba came to him in great agitation, and said they had fastened up the door, so that she could not get out. Curdie rose immediately and went with her: they found that not only the door, but every window in the house was so secured on the outside that it was impossible to open one of them without using great force. Poor Derba looked anxiously in Curdie's face. He broke out laughing.

'They are much mistaken,' he said, 'if they fancy they could keep Lina and a miner in any house in Gwyntystorm – even if they built up doors and windows.'

With that he shouldered his mattock. But Derba begged him not to make a hole in her house just yet. She had plenty for breakfast, she said, and before it was time for dinner they would know what the people meant by it.

And indeed they did. For within an hour appeared one of the chief magistrates of the city, accompanied by a score of soldiers with drawn swords, and followed by a great multitude of people, requiring the miner and his brute to yield themselves, the one that he might be tried for the disturbance he had occasioned and the injury he had committed, the other that she might be roasted alive for her part in killing two valuable and harmless animals belonging to worthy citizens. The summons was preceded and followed by flourish of trumpet, and was read with every formality by the city marshal himself.

The moment he ended, Lina ran into the little passage, and stood opposite the door.

'I surrender,' cried Curdie.

'Then tie up your brute, and give her here.'

'No, no,' cried Curdie through the door. 'I surrender; but I'm not going to do your hangman's work. If you want my dog, you must take her.'

'Then we shall set the house on fire, and burn witch and all.'

'It will go hard with us but we shall kill a few dozen of you first,' cried Curdie. 'We're not the least afraid of you.'

With that Curdie turned to Derba, and said:

'Don't be frightened. I have a strong feeling that all will be well. Surely no trouble will come to you for being good to strangers.'

'But the poor dog!' said Derba.

Now Curdie and Lina understood each other more than a little by this time, and not only had he seen that she understood the proclamation, but when she looked up at him after it was read, it was with such a grin, and such a yellow flash, that he saw also she was determined to take care of herself.

'The dog will probably give you reason to think a little more of her ere long,' he answered. 'But now,' he went on, 'I fear I must hurt your house a little. I have great confidence, however, that I shall be able to make up to you for it one day.'

'Never mind the house, if only you can get safe off,' she answered. 'I don't think they will hurt this precious lamb,' she added, clasping little Barbara to her bosom. 'For myself, it is all one; I am ready for anything.'

'It is but a little hole for Lina I want to make,' said Curdie. 'She can creep through a much smaller one than you would think.'

Again he took his mattock, and went to the back wall.

'They won't burn the house,' he said to himself. 'There is too good a one on each side of it.'

The tumult had kept increasing every moment, and the city marshal had been shouting, but Curdie had not listened to him. When now they heard the blows of his mattock, there went up a great cry, and the people taunted the soldiers that they were afraid of a dog and his miner. The soldiers therefore made a rush at the door, and cut its fastenings.

The moment they opened it, out leaped Lina, with a roar so unnaturally horrible that the sword arms of the soldiers dropped by their sides, paralysed with the terror of that cry; the crowd fled in every direction, shrieking and yelling with mortal dismay; and without even knocking down with her tail, not to say biting a man of them with her pulverizing jaws, Lina vanished — no one knew whither, for not one of the crowd had had courage to look upon her.

The moment she was gone, Curdie advanced and gave himself up. The soldiers were so filled with fear, shame, and chagrin, that they were ready to kill him on the spot. But he stood quietly facing them, with his mattock on his shoulder; and the magistrate wishing to examine him, and the people to see him made an example of, the soldiers had to content themselves with taking him. Partly for derision, partly to hurt him, they laid his mattock against his back, and tied his arms to it.

They led him up a very steep street, and up another still, all the crowd following. The king's palace-castle rose towering above them; but they stopped before they reached it, at a low-browed door in a great, dull, heavy-looking building.

The city marshal opened it with a key which hung at his girdle, and ordered Curdie to enter. The place within was dark as night, and while he was feeling his way with his feet, the marshal gave him a rough push. He fell, and rolled once or twice over, unable to help himself because his hands were tied behind him.

It was the hour of the magistrate's second and more important breakfast, and until that was over he never found himself capable of attending to a case with concentration sufficient to the distinguishing of the side upon which his own advantage lay; and hence was this respite for Curdie, with time to collect his thoughts. But indeed he had very few to collect, for all he had to do, so far as he could see, was to wait for what would come next. Neither had he much power to collect them, for he was a good deal shaken.

In a few minutes he discovered, to his great relief, that, from the projection of the pick end of his mattock beyond his body, the fall had loosened the ropes tied round it. He got one hand disengaged, and then the other; and presently stood free, with his good mattock once more in right serviceable relation to his arms and legs.

CHAPTER SIXTEEN

The Mattock

WHILE the magistrate reinvigorated his selfishness with a greedy breakfast, Curdie found doing nothing in the dark rather tiresome work. It was useless attempting to think what he should do next, seeing the circumstances in which he was presently to find himself were altogether unknown to him. So he began to think about his father and mother in their little cottage home, high in the clear air of the open mountainside, and the thought, instead of making his dungeon gloomier by the contrast, made a light in his soul that destroyed the power of darkness and captivity.

But he was at length startled from his waking dream by a swell in the noise outside. All the time there had been a few of the more idle of the inhabitants about the door, but they had been rather quiet. Now, however, the sounds of feet and voices began to grow, and grew so rapidly that it was plain a multitude was gathering. For the people of Gwyntystorm always gave themselves an hour of pleasure after their second breakfast, and what greater pleasure could they have than to see a stranger abused by the officers of justice?

The noise grew till it was like the roaring of the sea, and that roaring went on a long time, for the magistrate, being a great man, liked to know that he was waited for: it added to the enjoyment of his breakfast, and, indeed, enabled him to eat a little more after he had thought his powers exhausted. But at length, in the waves of the human noises rose a bigger wave, and by the running and shouting and outcry, Curdie learned that the magistrate was approaching.

Presently came the sound of the great rusty key in the lock, which yielded with groaning reluctance; the door was thrown back, the light rushed in, and with it came the voice of the city marshal, calling upon Curdie, by many legal epithets opprobrious, to come forth and be tried for his life, inasmuch as he had raised a tumult in His Majesty's city of Gwyntystorm, troubled the hearts of the king's baker and barber, and slain the faithful dogs of His Majesty's well-beloved butchers.

He was still reading, and Curdie was still seated in the brown twilight of the vault, not listening, but pondering with himself how this king the city marshal talked of could be the same with the Majesty he had seen ride away on his grand white horse with the Princess Irene on a cushion before him, when a scream of agonized terror arose on the farthest skirt of the crowd, and, swifter than flood or flame, the horror spread shrieking. In a moment the air was filled with hideous howling, cries of unspeakable dismay, and the multitudinous noise of running feet. The next moment, in at the door of the vault bounded Lina, her two green eyes flaming yellow as sunflowers, and seeming to light up the dungeon. With one spring she threw herself at Curdie's feet, and laid her head upon them panting. Then came a rush of two or three soldiers darkening the doorway, but it was only to lay hold of the key, pull the door to, and lock it; so that once more Curdie and

105

Lina were prisoners together.

For a few moments Lina lay panting hard: it is breathless work leaping and roaring both at once, and that in a way to scatter thousands of people. Then she jumped up, and began snuffing about all over the place; and Curdie saw what he had never seen before — two faint spots of light cast from her eyes upon the ground, one on each side of her snuffing nose. He got out his tinder box — a miner is never without one — and lighted a precious bit of candle he carried in a division of it, just for a moment, for he must not waste it.

The light revealed a vault without any window or other opening than the door. It was very old and much neglected. The mortar had vanished from between the stones, and it was half filled with a heap, of all sorts of rubbish, beaten down in the middle, but looser at the sides; it sloped from the door to the foot of the opposite wall: evidently for a long time the vault had been left open, and every sort of refuse thrown into it. A single minute served for the survey, so little was there to note.

Meantime, down in the angle between the back wall and the base of the heap Lina was scratching furiously with all the eighteen great strong claws of her mighty feet.

'Ah, ha!' said Curdie to himself, catching sight of her, 'only they will leave us long enough to ourselves!'

With that he ran to the door, to see if there was any fastening on the inside. There was none: in all its long history it never had had one. But a few blows of the right sort, now from the one, now from the other end of his mattock, were as good as any bolt, for they so ruined the lock that no key could ever turn in it again. Those who heard them fancied he was trying to get out, and laughed spitefully. As soon as he had done, he extinguished his candle, and went down to Lina.

She had reached the hard rock which formed the floor of the dungeon, and was now clearing away the earth a little wider. Presently she looked up in his face and whined, as much to say, 'My paws are not hard enough to get any farther.'

'Then get out of my way, Lina,' said Curdie, 'and mind you keep your eyes shining, for fear I should hit you.'

So saying, he heaved his mattock, and assailed with the hammer end of it the spot she had cleared.

The rock was very hard, but when it did break it broke in good-sized pieces. Now with hammer, now with pick, he worked till he was weary, then rested, and then set to again. He could not tell how the day went, as he had no light but the lamping of Lina's eyes. The darkness hampered him greatly, for he would not let Lina come close enough to give him all the light she could, lest he should strike her. So he had, every now and then, to feel with his hands to know how he was getting on, and to discover in what direction to strike: the exact spot was a mere imagination.

He was getting very tired and hungry, and beginning to lose heart a little, when out of the ground, as if he had struck a spring of it, burst a dull, gleamy, lead-coloured light, and the next moment he heard a hollow splash and echo. A piece of rock had fallen out of the floor, and dropped into water beneath. Already Lina, who had been lying a few yards off all the time he worked, was on her feet and peering through the hole. Curdie got down on his hands and knees, and looked. They were over what seemed a natural cave in the rock, to which apparently the river had access, for, at a great distance below, a faint light was gleaming upon water. If they could

107

but reach it, they might get out; but even if it was deep enough, the height was very dangerous. The first thing whatever might follow, was to make the hole larger. It was comparatively easy to break away the sides of it, and in the course of another hour he had it large enough to get through.

And now he must reconnoitre. He took the rope they had tied him with — for Curdie's hindrances were always his furtherance — and fastened one end of it by a slipknot round the handle of his pickaxe, then dropped the other end through, and laid the pickaxe so that, when he was through himself, and hanging on the edge, he could place it across the hole to support him on the rope. This done, he took the rope in his hands, and, beginning to descend, found himself in a narrow cleft widening into a cave. His rope was not very long, and would not do much to lessen the force of his fall — he thought to himself — if he should have to drop into the water; but he was not more than a couple of yards below the dungeon when he spied an opening on the opposite side of the cleft: it might be but a shadow hole, or it might lead them out. He dropped himself a little below its level, gave the rope a swing by pushing his feet against the side of the cleft, and so pendaled himself into it. Then he laid a stone on the end of the rope that it should not forsake him, called to Lina, whose yellow eyes were gleaming over the mattock grating above, to watch there till he returned, and went cautiously in.

It proved a passage, level for some distance, then sloping gently up. He advanced carefully, feeling his way as he went. At length he was stopped by a door — a small door, studded with iron. But the wood was in places so much decayed that some of the bolts had dropped out, and he felt sure of being able to open it. He returned, therefore, to fetch Lina and his mattock. Arrived at the cleft, his strong miner arms bore him swiftly up along the rope and through the hole into the dungeon. There he undid the rope from his mattock, and making Lina take the end of it in her teeth, and get through the hole, he lowered her – it was all he could do, she was so heavy. When she came opposite the passage, with a slight push of her tail she shot herself into it, and let go the rope, which Curdie drew up.

Then he lighted his candle and searching in the rubbish found a bit of iron to take the place of his pickaxe across the hole. Then he searched again in the rubbish, and found half an old shutter. This he propped up leaning a little over the hole, with a bit of stick, and heaped against the back of it a quantity of the loosened earth. Next he tied his mattock to the end of the rope, dropped it, and let it hang. Last, he got through the hole himself, and pulled away the propping stick, so that the shutter fell over the hole with a quantity of earth on the top of it. A few motions of hand over hand, and he swung himself and his mattock into the passage beside Lina. There he secured the end of the rope, and they went on together to the door.

CHAPTER SEVENTEEN

The Wine Cellar

He lighted his candle and examined it. Decayed and broken as it was, it was strongly secured in its place by hinges on the one side, and either lock or bolt, he could not tell which, on the other. A brief use of his pocket-knife was enough to make room for his hand and arm to get through, and then he found a great iron bolt – but so rusty that he could not move it. Lina whimpered. He took his knife again, made the hole bigger, and stood back. In she shot her small head and long neck, seized the bolt with her teeth, and dragged it, grating and complaining, back. A push then opened the door. It was at the foot of a short flight of steps. They ascended, and at the top Curdie found himself in a space which, from the echo to his stamp, appeared of some size, though of what sort he could not at first tell for his hands, feeling about, came upon nothing. Presently, however, they fell on a great thing: it was a wine cask.

He was just setting out to explore the place thoroughly, when he heard steps coming down a stair. He stood still, not knowing whether the door would open an inch from his nose or twenty yards behind his back. It did neither. He heard the key turn in the lock, and a stream of light shot in, ruining the darkness, about fifteen yards away on his right.

A man carrying a candle in one hand and a large silver flagon in the other, entered, and came toward him. The light revealed a row of huge wine casks, that stretched away into the darkness of the other end of the long vault. Curdie retreated into the recess of the stair, and peeping round the corner of it, watched him, thinking what he could do to prevent him from locking them in. He came on and on, until Curdie feared he would pass the recess and see them. He was just preparing to rush out, and master him before he should give alarm, not in the least knowing what he should do next, when, to his relief, the man stopped at the third cask from where he stood. He set down his light on the top of it, removed what seemed a large vent-peg, and poured into the cask a quantity of something from the flagon. Then he turned to the next cask, drew some wine, rinsed the flagon, threw the wine away, drew and rinsed and threw away again, then drew and drank, draining to the bottom. Last of all, he filled the flagon from the cask he had first visited, replaced then the vent-peg, took up his candle, and turned toward the door.

'There is something wrong here!' thought Curdie.

'Speak to him, Lina,' he whispered.

The sudden howl she gave made Curdie himself start and tremble for a moment. As to the man, he answered Lina's with another horrible howl, forced from him by the convulsive shudder of every muscle of his body, then reeled gasping to and fro, and dropped his candle. But just as Curdie expected to see him fall dead he recovered himself, and flew to the door, through which he darted, leaving it open behind him. The moment he ran, Curdie stepped out, picked up the candle still alight, sped after him to the door, drew out the key, and then returned to the stair and waited. In a few minutes he heard the sound of many feet and voices. Instantly he turned the tap of the cask from which the man had been drinking, set the candle beside it on the floor, went down the steps and out of the little door, followed by Lina, and closed it behind them.

Through the hole in it he could see a little, and hear all. He could see how the light of many candles filled the place, and could hear how some two dozen feet ran hither and thither through the echoing cellar; he could hear the clash of iron, probably spits and pokers, now and then; and at last heard how, finding nothing remarkable except the best wine running to waste, they all turned on the butler and accused him of having fooled them with a drunken dream. He did his best to defend himself, appealing to the evidence of their own senses that he was as sober as they were. They replied that a fright was no less a fright that the cause was imaginary, and a dream no less a dream that the fright had waked him from it.

When he discovered, and triumphantly adduced as corroboration, that the key was gone from the door, they said it merely showed how drunk he had been — either that or how frightened, for he had certainly dropped it. In vain he protested that he had never taken it out of the lock — that he never did when he went in, and certainly had not this time stopped to do so when he came out; they asked him why he had to go to the cellar at such a time of the day, and said it was because he had already drunk all the wine that was left from dinner. He said if he had dropped the key, the key was to be found, and they must help him to find it. They told him they wouldn't move a peg for him. He declared, with much language, he would have them all turned out of the king's service. They said they would swear he was drunk.

And so positive were they about it, that at last the butler himself began to think whether it was possible they could be in the right. For he knew that sometimes when he had been drunk he fancied things had taken place which he found afterward could not have happened. Certain of his fellow servants, however, had all the time a doubt whether the cellar goblin had not appeared to him, or at least roared at him, to protect the wine. In any case nobody wanted to find the key for him; nothing could please them better than that the door of the wine cellar should never more be locked. By degrees the hubbub died away, and they departed, not even pulling to the door, for there was neither handle nor latch to it.

As soon as they were gone, Curdie returned, knowing now that they were in the wine cellar of the palace, as indeed, he had suspected. Finding a pool of wine in a hollow of the floor, Lina lapped it up eagerly: she had had no breakfast, and was now very thirsty as well as hungry. Her master was in a similar plight, for he had but just begun to eat when the magistrate arrived with the soldiers. If only they were all in bed, he thought, that he might find his way to the larder! For he said to himself that, as he was sent there by the young princess's great-great-grandmother to serve her or her father in some way, surely he must have a right to his food in the palace, without which he could do nothing. He would go at once and reconnoitre.

So he crept up the stair that led from the cellar. At the top was a door, opening on a long passage dimly lighted by a lamp. He told Lina to lie down upon the stair while he went on. At the end of the passage he found a door ajar, and, peering through, saw right into a great stone hall, where a huge fire was blazing, and through which men in the king's livery were constantly coming and going. Some also in the same livery were lounging about the fire. He noted that their colours were the same as those he himself, as king's miner, wore; but from what he had seen and heard of the habits of the place, he could not hope they would treat him the better for that.

The one interesting thing at the moment however, was the plentiful supper with which the table was spread. It was something at least to stand in sight of food, and he was unwilling to turn his back on the prospect so long as a share in it was not absolutely hopeless. Peeping thus, he soon made up his mind that if at any moment the hall should be empty, he would at that moment rush in and attempt to carry off a dish. That he might lose no time by indecision, he selected a large pie upon which to pounce instantaneously. But after he had watched for some minutes, it did not seem at all likely the chance would arrive before suppertime, and he was just about to turn away and rejoin Lina, when he saw that there was not a person in the place. Curdie never made up his mind and then hesitated. He darted in, seized the pie, and bore it swiftly and noiselessly to the cellar stair.

CHAPTER EIGHTEEN

The King's Kitchen

BACK to the cellar Curdie and Lina sped with their booty, where, seated on the steps, Curdie lighted his bit of candle for a moment. A very little bit it was now, but they did not waste much of it in examination of the pie; that they effected by a more summary process. Curdie thought it the nicest food he had ever tasted, and between them they soon ate it up. Then Curdie would have thrown the dish along with the bones into the water, that there might be no traces of them; but he thought of his mother, and hid it instead; and the very next minute they wanted it to draw some wine into. He was careful it should be from the cask of which he had seen the butler drink.

Then they sat down again upon the steps, and waited until the house should be quiet. For he was there to do something, and if it did not come to him in the cellar, he must go to meet it in other places. Therefore, lest he should fall asleep, he set the end of the helve of his mattock on the ground, and seated himself on the cross part, leaning against the wall, so that as long as he kept awake he should rest, but the moment he began to fall asleep he must fall awake instead. He quite expected some of the servants would visit the cellar again that night, but whether it was that they were afraid of each other, or believed more of the butler's story than they had chosen to allow, not one of them appeared.

When at length he thought he might venture, he shouldered his mattock and crept up the stair. The lamp was out in the passage, but he could not miss his way to the servants' hall. Trusting to Lina's quickness in concealing herself, he took her with him.

When they reached the hall they found it quiet and nearly dark. The last of the great fire was glowing red, but giving little light. Curdie stood and warmed himself for a few moments: miner as he was, he had found the cellar cold to sit in doing nothing; and standing thus he thought of looking if there were any bits of candle about. There were many candlesticks on the supper table, but to his disappointment and indignation their candles seemed to have been all left to burn out, and some of them, indeed, he found still hot in the neck.

Presently, one after another, he came upon seven men fast asleep, most of them upon tables, one in a chair, and one on the floor. They seemed, from their shape and colour, to have eaten and drunk so much that they might be burned alive without waking. He grasped the hand of each in succession, and found two ox hoofs, three pig hoofs, one concerning which he could not be sure whether it was the hoof of a donkey or a pony, and one dog's paw. 'A nice set of people to be about a king!' thought Curdie to himself, and turned again to his candle hunt. He did at last find two or three little pieces, and stowed them away in his pockets.

They now left the hall by another door, and entered a short passage, which led them to the huge kitchen, vaulted and black with smoke. There, too, the fire was still burning, so that he was able to see a little of the state of things in this quarter also. The place was dirty and disorderly. In a recess, on a heap of brushwood, lay a kitchenmaid, with a table cover around her, and a skillet in her hand: evidently she too had been drinking. In another corner lay a page, and Curdie noted how like his dress was to his own. In the cinders before the hearth were huddled three dogs and five cats, all fast asleep, while the rats were running about the floor. Curdie's heart ached to think of the lovely child-princess living over such a sty. The mine was a paradise to a palace with such servants in it.

Leaving the kitchen, he got into the region of the sculleries. There horrible smells were wandering about, like evil spirits that came forth with the darkness. He lighted a candle — but only to see ugly sights. Everywhere was filth and disorder. Mangy turnspit dogs were lying about, and grey rats were gnawing at refuse in the sinks. It was like a hideous dream. He felt as if he should never get out of it, and longed for one glimpse of his mother's poor little kitchen, so clean and bright and airy. Turning from it at last in miserable disgust, he almost ran back through the kitchen, re-entered the hall, and crossed it to another door.

It opened upon a wider passage leading to an arch in a stately corridor, all its length lighted by lamps in niches. At the end of it was a large and beautiful hall, with great pillars. There sat three men in the royal livery, fast asleep, each in a great armchair, with his feet on a huge footstool. They looked like fools dreaming themselves kings; and Lina looked as if she longed to throttle them. At one side of the hall was the grand staircase, and they went up.

Everything that now met Curdie's eyes was rich — not

glorious like the splendours of the mountain cavern, but rich and soft – except where, now and then, some rough old rib of the ancient fortress came through, hard and discoloured. Now some dark bare arch of stone, now some rugged and blackened pillar, now some huge beam, brown with the smoke and dust of centuries, looked like a thistle in the midst of daisies, or a rock in a smooth lawn.

They wandered about a good while, again and again finding themselves where they had been before. Gradually, however, Curdie was gaining some idea of the place. By and by Lina began to look frightened, and as they went on Curdie saw that she looked more and more frightened. Now, by this time he had come to understand that what made her look frightened was always the fear of frightening, and he therefore concluded they must be drawing nigh to somebody.

At last, in a gorgeously painted gallery, he saw a curtain of crimson, and on the curtain a royal crown wrought in silks and stones. He felt sure this must be the king's chamber, and it was here he was wanted: or, if it was not the place he was bound for, something would meet him and turn him aside; for he had come to think that so long as a man wants to do right he may go where he can: when he can go no farther, then it is not the way. 'Only,' said his father, in assenting to the theory, 'he must really want to do right, and not merely fancy he does. He must want it with his heart and will, and not with his rag of a tongue.'

So he gently lifted the corner of the curtain, and there behind it was a half-open door. He entered, and the moment he was in, Lina stretched along the threshold between the curtain and the door.

CHAPTER NINETEEN

The King's Chamber

HE found himself in a large room, dimly lighted by a silver lamp that hung from the ceiling. Far at the other end was a great bed, surrounded with dark heavy curtains. He went softly toward it, his heart beating fast. It was a dreadful thing to be alone in the king's chamber at the dead of night. To gain courage he had to remind himself of the beautiful princess who had sent him.

But when he was about halfway to the bed, a figure appeared from the farther side of it, and came towards him, with a hand raised warningly. He stood still. The light was dim, and he could distinguish little more than the outline of a young girl. But though the form he saw was much taller than the princess he remembered, he never doubted it was she. For one thing, he knew that most girls would have been frightened to see him there in the dead of the night, but like a true princess, and the princess he used to know, she walked straight on to meet him. As she came she lowered the hand she had lifted and laid the forefinger of it upon her lips. Nearer and nearer, quite near, close up to him she came, then stopped, and stood a moment looking at him.

'You are Curdie,' she said.

'And you are the Princess Irene,' he returned.

'Then we know each other still,' she said, with a sad smile of pleasure. 'You will help me.'

'That I will,' answered Curdie. He did not say, 'If I can'; for he knew that what he was sent to do, that he could do. 'May I kiss your hand, little Princess?'

She was only between nine and ten, though indeed she looked several years older, and her eyes almost those of a grown woman, for she had had terrible trouble of late.

She held out her hand.

'I am not the *little* princess any more. I have grown up since I saw you last, Mr Miner.'

The smile which accompanied the words had in it a strange mixture of playfulness and sadness.

'So I see, Miss Princess,' returned Curdie; 'and therefore, being more of a princess, you are the more my princess. Here I am, sent by your great-great-grandmother, to be your servant. May I ask why you are up so late, Princess?'

'Because my father wakes *so* frightened, and I don't know what he *would* do if he didn't find me by his bedside. There! he's waking now.'

She darted off to the side of the bed she had come from. Curdie stood where he was.

A voice altogether unlike what he remembered of the mighty, noble king on his white horse came from the bed, thin, feeble, hollow, and husky, and in tone like that of a petulant child:

'I will not, I will not. I am a king, and I *will* be a king. I hate you and despise you, and you shall not torture me!'

'Never mind them, Father dear,' said the princess. 'I am here, and they sha'n't touch you. They dare not, you know, so long as you defy them.'

'They want my crown, darling; and I can't give them my crown, can I? For what is a king without his crown?'

'They shall never have your crown, my king,' said Irene. 'Here it is — all safe. I am watching it for you.'

Curdie drew near the bed on the other side. There lay the grand old king — he looked grand still, and twenty years older. His body was pillowed high; his beard descended long and white over the crimson coverlid; and his crown, its diamonds and emeralds gleaming in the twilight of the curtains, lay in front of him, his long thin old hands folded round it, and the ends of his beard straying among lovely stones. His face was like that of a man who had died fighting nobly; but one thing made it dreadful: his eyes, while they moved about as if searching in this direction and in that, looked more dead than his face. He saw neither his daughter nor his crown: it was the voice of the one and the touch of the other that comforted him. He kept murmuring what seemed words, but was unintelligible to Curdie, although, to judge from the look of Irene's face, she learned and concluded from it.

By degrees his voice sank away and the murmuring ceased, although still his lips moved. Thus lay the old king on his bed, slumbering with his crown between his hands; on one side of him stood a lovely little maiden, with blue eyes, and brown hair going a little back from her temples, as if blown by a wind that no one felt but herself; and on the other a stalwart young miner, with his mattock over his shoulder. Stranger sight still was Lina lying along the threshold — only nobody saw her just then.

A moment more and the king's lips ceased to move. His

121

breathing had grown regular and quiet. The princess gave a sigh of relief, and came round to Curdie.

'We can talk a little now,' she said, leading him toward the middle of the room. 'My father will sleep now till the doctor wakes him to give him his medicine. It is not really medicine, though, but wine. Nothing but that, the doctor says, could have kept him so long alive. He always comes in the middle of the night to give it him with his own hands. But it makes me cry to see him wake up when so nicely asleep.'

'What sort of man is your doctor?' asked Curdie.

'Oh, such a dear, good, kind gentleman!' replied the princess. 'He speaks so softly, and is so sorry for his dear king! He will be here presently, and you shall see for yourself. You will like him very much.'

'Has your king-father been long ill?' asked Curdie.

'A whole year now,' she replied. 'Did you not know? That's how your mother never got the red petticoat my father promised her. The lord chancellor told me that not only Gwyntystorm but the whole land was mourning over the illness of the good man.'

Now Curdie himself had not heard a word of His Majesty's illness, and had no ground for believing that a single soul in any place he had visited on his journey had heard of it. Moreover, although mention had been made of His Majesty again and again in his hearing since he came to Gwyntystorm, never once had he heard an allusion to the state of his health. And now it dawned upon him also that he had never heard the least expression of love to him. But just for the time he thought it better to say nothing on either point.

'Does the king wander like this every night?' he asked.

'Every night,' answered Irene, shaking her head

mournfully. 'That is why I never go to bed at night. He is better during the day – a little, and then I sleep – in the dressing room there, to be with him in a moment if he should call me. It is *so* sad he should have only me and not my mamma! A princess is nothing to a queen!'

'I wish he would like me,' said Curdie 'for then I might watch by him at night, and let you go to bed, Princess.'

'Don't you know then?' returned Irene, in wonder. 'How was it you came? Ah! You said my grandmother sent you. But I thought you knew that he wanted you.'

And again she opened wide her blue stars.

'Not I,' said Curdie, also bewildered, but very glad.

'He used to be constantly saying – he was not so ill then as he is now – that he wished he had you about him.'

'And I never to know it!' said Curdie, with displeasure.

'The master of the horse told papa's own secretary that he had written to the miner-general to find you and send you up; but the miner-general wrote back to the master of the horse, and he told the secretary, and the secretary told my father, that they had searched every mine in the kingdom and could hear nothing of you. My father gave a great sigh, and said he feared the goblins had got you, after all, and your father and mother were dead of grief. And he has never mentioned you since, except when wandering. I cried very much. But one of my grandmother's pigeons with its white wing flashed a message to me through the window one day, and then I knew that my Curdie wasn't eaten by the goblins, for my grandmother wouldn't have taken care of him one time to let him be eaten the next. Where were you, Curdie, that they couldn't find you?'

'We will talk about that another time, when we are not

123

expecting the doctor,' said Curdie.

As he spoke, his eyes fell upon something shining on the table under the lamp. His heart gave a great throb, and he went nearer. Yes, there could bed no doubt — it was the same flagon that the butler had filled in the wine cellar.

'It looks worse and worse!' he said to himself, and went back to Irene, where she stood half dreaming.

'When will the doctor be here?' he asked once more — this time hurriedly.

The question was answered — not by the princess, but by something which that instant tumbled heavily into the room. Curdie flew toward it in vague terror about Lina.

On the floor lay a little round man, puffing and blowing and uttering incoherent language. Curdie thought of his mattock, and ran and laid it aside.

'Oh, dear Dr Kelman!' cried the princess, running up and taking hold of his arm; 'I am *so* sorry!' She pulled and pulled, but might almost as well have tried to set up a cannon ball. 'I hope you have not hurt yourself?'

'Not at all, not at all,' said the doctor, trying to smile and to rise both at once, but finding it impossible to do either.

'If he slept on the floor he would be late for breakfast,' said Curdie to himself, and held out his hand to help him.

But when he took hold of it, Curdie very nearly let him fall again, for what he held was not even a foot: it was the belly of a creeping thing. He managed, however, to hold both his peace and his grasp, and pulled the doctor roughly on his legs — such as they were.

'Your Royal Highness has rather a thick mat at the door,' said the doctor, patting his palms together. 'I hope my awkwardness may not have startled His Majesty.'

While he talked Curdie went to the door: Lina was not there.

The doctor approached the bed.

'And how has my beloved king slept tonight?' he asked.

'No better,' answered Irene, with a mournful shake of her head.

'Ah, that is very well!' returned the doctor, his fall seeming to have muddled either his words or his meaning. 'When we give him his wine, he will be better still.'

Curdie darted at the flagon, and lifted it high, as if he had expected to find it full, but had found it empty.

'That stupid butler! I heard them say he was drunk!' he cried in a loud whisper, and was gliding from the room.

'Come here with that flagon, you! Page!' cried the doctor.

Curdie came a few steps toward him with the flagon dangling from his hand, heedless of the gushes that fell noiseless on the thick carpet.

'Are you aware, young man,' said the doctor, 'that it is not every wine can do His Majesty the benefit I intend he should derive from my prescription?'

'Quite aware, sir,' answered Curdie. 'The wine for His Majesty's use is in the third cask from the corner.'

'Fly, then,' said the doctor, looking satisfied.

Curdie stopped outside the curtain and blew an audible breath – no more; up came Lina noiseless as a shadow. He showed her the flagon.

'The cellar, Lina: go,' he said.

She galloped away on her soft feet, and Curdie had indeed to fly to keep up with her. Not once did she make even a dubious turn. From the king's gorgeous chamber to the cold cellar they shot. Curdie dashed the wine down the back stair,

125

rinsed the flagon out as he had seen the butler do, filled it from the cask of which he had seen the butler drink, and hastened with it up again to the king's room.

The little doctor took it, poured out a full glass, smelt, but did not taste it, and set it down. Then he leaned over the bed, shouted in the king's ear, blew upon his eyes, and pinched his arm: Curdie thought he saw him run something bright into it. At last the king half woke. The doctor seized the glass, raised his head, poured the wine down his throat, and let his head fall back on the pillow again. Tenderly wiping his beard, and bidding the princess good night in paternal tones, he then took his leave. Curdie would gladly have driven his pick into his head, but that was not in his commission, and he let him go.

The little round man looked very carefully to his feet as he crossed the threshold.

'That attentive fellow of a page has removed the mat,' he said to himself, as he walked along the corridor. 'I must remember him.'

CHAPTER TWENTY

Counterplotting

CURDIE was already sufficiently enlightened as to how things were going, to see he must have the princess of one mind with him, and they must work together. It was clear that among those about the king there was a plot against him: for one thing, they had agreed in a lie concerning himself; and it was plain also that the doctor was working out a design against the health and reason of His Majesty, rendering the question of his life a matter of little moment. It was in itself sufficient to justify the worst fears, that the people outside the place were ignorant of His Majesty's condition: he believed those inside it also — the butler excepted — were ignorant of it as well. Doubtless His Majesty's councillors desired to alienate the hearts of his subjects from their sovereign. Curdie's idea was that they intended to kill the king, marry the princess to one of themselves, and found a new dynasty; but whatever their purpose, there was treason in the palace of the worst sort: they were making and keeping the king incapable, in order to effect that purpose. The first thing to be seen to, therefore, was that His Majesty should neither eat morsel nor drink drop of anything prepared for him in the palace. Could this have been managed without the princess, Curdie would have preferred leaving her in ignorance of the horrors from which he sought to deliver her. He feared also the danger of her knowledge betraying itself to the evil eyes about her; but it must be risked – and she had always been a wise child.

Another thing was clear to him – that with such traitors no terms of honour were either binding or possible, and that, short of lying, he might use any means to foil them. And he could not doubt that the old princess had sent him expressly to frustrate their plans.

While he stood thinking thus with himself, the princess was earnestly watching the king, with looks of childish love and womanly tenderness that went to Curdie's heart. Now and then with a great fan of peacock feathers she would fan him very softly; now and then, seeing a cloud begin to gather upon the sky of his sleeping face, she would climb upon the bed, and bending to his ear whisper into it, then draw back and watch again – generally to see the cloud disperse. In his deepest slumber, the soul of the king lay open to the voice of his child, and that voice had power either to change the aspect of his visions, or, which was better still, to breathe hope into his heart, and courage to endure them.

Curdie came near, and softly called her.

'I can't leave Papa just yet,' she returned, in a low voice.

'I will wait,' said Curdie; 'but I want very much to say something.'

In a few minutes she came to him where he stood under the lamp.

'Well, Curdie, what is it?' she said.

'Princess,' he replied, 'I want to tell you that I have found why your grandmother sent me.'

'Come this way, then,' she answered, 'where I can see the

face of my king.'

Curdie placed a chair for her in the spot she chose, where she would be near enough to mark any slightest change on her father's countenance, yet where their low-voiced talk would not disturb him. There he sat down beside her and told her all the story — how her grandmother had sent her good pigeon for him, and how she had instructed him, and sent him there without telling him what he had to do. Then he told her what he had discovered of the state of things generally in Gwyntystorm, and especially what he had heard and seen in the palace that night.

'Things are in a bad state enough,' he said in conclusion — 'lying and selfishness and inhospitality and dishonesty everywhere; and to crown all, they speak with disrespect of the good king, and not a man knows he is ill.'

'You frighten me dreadfully,' said Irene, trembling.

'You must be brave for your king's sake,' said Curdie.

'Indeed I will,' she replied, and turned a long loving look upon the beautiful face of her father. 'But what *is* to be done? And how *am* I to believe such horrible things of Dr Kelman?'

'My dear Princess,' replied Curdie, 'you know nothing of him but his face and his tongue, and they are both false. Either you must beware of him, or you must doubt your grandmother and me; for I tell you, by the gift she gave me of testing hands, that this man is a snake. That round body he shows is but the case of a serpent. Perhaps the creature lies there, as in its nest, coiled round and round inside.'

'Horrible!' said Irene.

'Horrible indeed; but we must not try to get rid of horrible things by refusing to look at them, and saying they are not there. Is not your beautiful father sleeping better since he had

129

the wine?'

'Yes.'

'Does he always sleep better after having it?'

She reflected an instant.

'No; always worse — till tonight,' she answered.

'Then remember that was the wine I got him — not what the butler drew. Nothing that passes through any hand in the house except yours or mine must henceforth, till he is well, reach His Majesty's lips.'

'But how, dear Curdie?' said the princess, almost crying.

'That we must contrive,' answered Curdie. 'I know how to take care of the wine; but for his food — now we must think.'

'He takes hardly any,' said the princess, with a pathetic shake of her little head which Curdie had almost learned to look for.

'The more need,' he replied, 'there should be no poison in it.' Irene shuddered. 'As soon as he has honest food he will begin to grow better. And you must be just as careful with yourself, Princess,' Curdie went on, 'for you don't know when they may begin to poison you, too.'

'There's no fear of me; don't talk about me,' said Irene. 'The good food! How are we to get it, Curdie? That is the whole question.'

'I am thinking hard,' answered Curdie. 'The good food? Let me see — let me see! Such servants as I saw below are sure to have the best of everything for themselves: I will go and see what I can find on their table.'

'The chancellor sleeps in the house, and he and the master of the king's horse always have their supper together in a room off the great hall, to the right as you go down the stairs,' said Irene. 'I would go with you, but I dare not leave my father.

Alas! He scarcely ever takes more than a mouthful. I can't think how he lives! And the very thing he would like, and often asks for — a bit of bread — I can hardly ever get for him: Dr Kelman has forbidden it, and says it is nothing less than poison to him.'

'Bread at least he *shall* have,' said Curdie; 'and that, with the honest wine, will do as well as anything, I do believe. I will go at once and look for some. But I want you to see Lina first, and know her, lest, coming upon her by accident at any time, you should be frightened.'

'I should like much to see her,' said the princess.

Warning her not to be startled by her ugliness, he went to the door and called her.

She entered, creeping with downcast head, and dragging her tail over the floor behind her. Curdie watched the princess as the frightful creature came nearer and nearer. One shudder went from head to foot, and next instant she stepped to meet her. Lina dropped flat on the floor, and covered her face with her two big paws. It went to the heart of the princess: in a moment she was on her knees beside her, stroking her ugly head, and patting her all over.

'Good dog! Dear ugly dog!' she said.

Lina whimpered.

'I believe,' said Curdie, 'from what your grandmother told me, that Lina is a woman, and that she was naughty, but is now growing good.'

Lina had lifted her head while Irene was caressing her; now she dropped it again between her paws; but the princess took it in her hands, and kissed the forehead betwixt the gold-green eyes.

'Shall I take her with me or leave her?' asked Curdie.

'Leave her, poor dear,' said Irene, and Curdie, knowing the way now, went without her.

He took his way first to the room the princess had spoken of, and there also were the remains of supper; but neither there nor in the kitchen could he find a scrap of plain wholesome-looking bread. So he returned and told her that as soon as it was light he would go into the city for some, and asked her for a handkerchief to tie it in. If he could not bring it himself, he would send it by Lina, who could keep out of sight better than he, and as soon as all was quiet at night he would come to her again. He also asked her to tell the king that he was in the house.

His hope lay in the fact that bakers everywhere go to work early. But it was yet much too early. So he persuaded the princess to lie down, promising to call her if the king should stir.

CHAPTER TWENTY-ONE

The Loaf

HIS Majesty slept very quietly. The dawn had grown almost day, and still Curdie lingered, unwilling to disturb the princess.

At last, however, he called her, and she was in the room in a moment. She had slept, she said, and felt quite fresh. Delighted to find her father still asleep, and so peacefully, she pushed her chair close to the bed, and sat down with her hands in her lap.

Curdie got his mattock from where he had hidden it behind a great mirror, and went to the cellar, followed by Lina. They took some breakfast with them as they passed through the hall, and as soon as they had eaten it went out the back way.

At the mouth of the passage Curdie seized the rope, drew himself up, pushed away the shutter, and entered the dungeon. Then he swung the end of the rope to Lina, and she caught it in her teeth. When her master said, 'Now, Lina!' she gave a great spring, and he ran away with the end of the rope as fast as ever he could. And such a spring had she made, that by the time he had to bear her weight she was within a few feet of the hole. The instant she got a paw through, she was all through.

Apparently their enemies were waiting till hunger should have cowed them, for there was no sign of any attempt having been made to open the door. A blow or two of Curdie's mattock drove the shattered lock clean from it, and telling Lina to wait there till he came back, and let no one in, he walked out into the silent street, and drew the door to behind them. He could hardly believe it was not yet a whole day since he had been thrown in there with his hands tied at his back.

Down the town he went, walking in the middle of the street, that, if any one saw him, he might see he was not afraid, and hesitate to rouse an attack on him. As to the dogs, ever since the death of their two companions, a shadow that looked like a mattock was enough to make them scamper. As soon as he reached the archway of the city gate he turned to reconnoitre the baker's shop, and perceiving no sign of movement, waited there watching for the first.

After about an hour, the door opened, and the baker's man appeared with a pail in his hand. He went to a pump that stood in the street, and having filled his pail returned with it into the shop. Curdie stole after him, found the door on the latch, opened it very gently, peeped in, saw nobody, and entered. Remembering perfectly from what shelf the baker's wife had taken the loaf she said was the best, and seeing just one upon it, he seized it, laid the price of it on the counter, and sped softly out, and up the street. Once more in the dungeon beside Lina, his first thought was to fasten up the door again, which would have been easy, so many iron fragments of all sorts and sizes lay about; but he bethought himself that if he left it as it was, and they came to find him, they would conclude at once that they had made their escape by it, and would look no farther so as to discover the hole. He therefore merely pushed the door close and left it. Then once more carefully arranging the earth behind the shutter, so that it should again fall with it, he returned to the cellar.

And now he had to convey the loaf to the princess. If he could venture to take it himself, well; if not, he would send Lina. He crept to the door of the servants' hall, and found the sleepers beginning to stir. One said it was time to go to bed; another, that he would go to the cellar instead, and have a mug of wine to waken him up; while a third challenged a fourth to give him his revenge at some game or other.

'Oh, hang your losses!' answered his companion; 'you'll soon pick up twice as much about the house, if you but keep your eyes open.'

Perceiving there would be risk in attempting to pass through, and reflecting that the porters in the great hall would probably be awake also, Curdie went back to the cellar, took Irene's handkerchief with the loaf in it, tied it round Lina's neck, and told her to take it to the princess.

Using every shadow and every shelter, Lina slid through the servants like a shapeless terror through a guilty mind, and so, by corridor and great hall, up the stair to the king's chamber.

Irene trembled a little when she saw her glide soundless in across the silent dusk of the morning, that filtered through the heavy drapery of the windows, but she recovered herself at once when she saw the bundle about her neck, for it both assured her of Curdie's safety, and gave her hope of her father's. She untied it with joy, and Lina stole away, silent as she had come. Her joy was the greater that the king had waked up a little before, and expressed a desire for food — not that he felt exactly hungry, he said, and yet he wanted some-

135

thing. If only he might have a piece of nice fresh bread! Irene had no knife, but with eager hands she broke a great piece from the loaf, and poured out a full glass of wine. The king ate and drank, enjoyed the bread and the wine much, and instantly fell asleep again.

It was hours before the lazy people brought their breakfast. When it came, Irene crumbled a little about, threw some into the fireplace, and managed to make the tray look just as usual.

In the meantime, down below in the cellar, Curdie was lying in the hollow between the upper sides of two of the great casks, the warmest place he could find. Lina was watching. She lay at his feet, across the two casks, and did her best so to arrange her huge tail that it should be a warm coverlid for her master.

By and by Dr Kelman called to see his patient; and now that Irene's eyes were opened, she saw clearly enough that he was both annoyed and puzzled at finding His Majesty rather better. He pretended however to congratulate him, saying he believed he was quite fit to see the lord chamberlain: he wanted his signature to something important; only he must not strain his mind to understand it, whatever it might be: if His Majesty did, he would not be answerable for the consequences. The king said he would see the lord chamberlain, and the doctor went.

Then Irene gave him more bread and wine, and the king ate and drank, and smiled a feeble smile, the first real one she had seen for many a day. He said he felt much better, and would soon be able to take matters into his own hands again. He had a strange miserable feeling, he said, that things were going terribly wrong, although he could not tell how. Then the princess told him that Curdie had come, and that at night, when all was quiet for nobody in the palace must know, he would pay His Majesty a visit. Her great-great-grandmother had sent him, she said. The king looked strangely upon her, but the strange look passed into a smile clearer than the first, and Irene's heart throbbed with delight.

CHAPTER TWENTY-TWO

The Lord Chamberlain

AT noon the lord chamberlain appeared. With a long, low bow, and paper in hand, he stepped softly into the room. Greeting His Majesty with every appearance of the profoundest respect, and congratulating him on the evident progress he had made, he declared himself sorry to trouble him, but there were certain papers, he said, which required his signature — and therewith drew nearer to the king, who lay looking at him doubtfully. He was a lean, long, yellow man, with a small head, bald over the top, and tufted at the back and about the ears. He had a very thin, prominent, hooked nose, and a quantity of loose skin under his chin and about the throat, which came craning up out of his neckcloth. His eyes were very small, sharp, and glittering, and looked black as jet. He had hardly enough of a mouth to make a smile with. His left hand held the paper, and the long, skinny fingers of his right a pen just dipped in ink.

But the king, who for weeks had scarcely known what he did, was today so much himself as to be aware that he was not quite himself; and the moment he saw the paper, he resolved that he would not sign without understanding and approving of it. He requested the lord chamberlain therefore to read it.

His Lordship commenced at once but the difficulties he seemed to encounter, and the fits of stammering that seized him, roused the king's suspicion tenfold. He called the princess.

'I trouble His Lordship too much,' he said to her: 'you can read print well, my child — let me hear how you can read writing. Take that paper from His Lordship's hand, and read it to me from beginning to end, while my lord drinks a glass of my favourite wine, and watches for your blunders.'

'Pardon me, Your Majesty,' said the lord chamberlain, with as much of a smile as he was able to extemporize, 'but it were a thousand pities to put the attainments of Her Royal Highness to a test altogether too severe. Your Majesty can scarcely with justice expect the very organs of her speech to prove capable of compassing words so long, and to her so unintelligible.'

'I think much of my little princess and her capabilities,' returned the king, more and more aroused. 'Pray, my lord, permit her to try.'

'Consider, Your Majesty: the thing would be altogether without precedent. It would be to make sport of statecraft,' said the lord chamberlain.

'Perhaps you are right, my lord,' answered the king, with more meaning than he intended should be manifest, while to his growing joy he felt new life and power throbbing in heart and brain. 'So this morning we shall read no further. I am indeed ill able for business of such weight.'

'Will Your Majesty please sign your royal name here?' said the lord chamberlain, preferring the request as a matter of course, and approaching with the feather end of the pen pointed to a spot where there was a great red seal.

'Not today, my lord,' replied the king.

'It is of the greatest importance, Your Majesty,' softl
insisted the other.

'I descried no such importance in it,' said the king.

'Your Majesty heard but a part.'

'And I can hear no more today.'

'I trust Your Majesty has ground enough, in a case c
necessity like the present, to sign upon the representation c
his loyal subject and chamberlain? Or shall I call the lor
chancellor?' he added, rising.

'There is no need. I have the very highest opinion of you
judgement, my lord,' answered the king; 'that is, with respec
to means: we *might* differ as to ends.'

The lord chamberlain made yet further attempts at persua
sion; but they grew feebler and feebler, and he was at las
compelled to retire without having gained his object. An
well might his annoyance be keen! For that paper was th
king's will, drawn up by the attorney-general; nor until the
had the king's signature to it was there much use in venturin
farther. But his worst sense of discomfiture arose from findin
the king with so much capacity left, for the doctor ha
pledged himself so to weaken his brain that he should be as
child in their hands, incapable of refusing anything requeste
of him: His Lordship began to doubt the doctor's fidelity t
the conspiracy.

The princess was in high delight. She had not for week
heard so many words, not to say words of such strength an
reason, from her father's lips: day by day he had bee
growing weaker and more lethargic. He was so mucl
exhausted, however, after this effort, that he asked for anothe
piece of bread and more wine, and fell fast asleep the momen
he had taken them.

The lord chamberlain sent in a rage for Dr Kelman. He came, and while professing himself unable to understand the symptoms described by His Lordship, yet pledged himself again that on the morrow the king should do whatever was required of him.

The day went on. When His Majesty was awake, the princess read to him — one storybook after another; and whatever she read, the king listened as if he had never heard anything so good before, making out in it the wisest meanings. Every now and then he asked for a piece of bread and a little wine, and every time he ate and drank he slept, and every time he woke he seemed better than the last time. The princess bearing her part, the loaf was eaten up and the flagon emptied before night. The butler took the flagon away, and brought it back filled to the brim, but both were thirsty and hungry when Curdie came again.

Meantime he and Lina, watching and waking alternately, had plenty of sleep. In the afternoon, peeping from the recess, they saw several of the servants enter hurriedly, one after the other, draw wine, drink it, and steal out; but their business was to take care of the king, not of his cellar, and they let them drink. Also, when the butler came to fill the flagon, they restrained themselves, for the villain's fate was not yet ready for him. He looked terribly frightened, and had brought with him a large candle and a small terrier — which latter indeed threatened to be troublesome, for he went roving and sniffing about until he came to the recess where they were. But as soon as he showed himself, Lina opened her jaws so wide, and glared at him so horribly, that, without even uttering a whimper, he tucked his tail between his legs and ran to his master. He was drawing the wicked wine at the moment, and did not see him, else he would doubtless have run too.

When suppertime approached, Curdie took his place at the door into the servants' hall; but after a long hour's vain watch, he began to fear he should get nothing: there was so much idling about, as well as coming and going. It was hard to bear — chiefly from the attractions of a splendid loaf, just fresh out of the oven, which he longed to secure for the king and princess. At length his chance did arrive: he pounced upon the loaf and carried it away, and soon after got hold of a pie.

This time, however, both loaf and pie were missed. The cook was called. He declared he had provided both. One of themselves, he said, must have carried them away for some friend outside the palace. Then a housemaid, who had not long been one of them, said she had seen someone like a page running in the direction of the cellar with something in his hands. Instantly all turned upon the pages, accusing them, one after another. All denied, but nobody believed one of them: where there is no truth there can be no faith.

To the cellar they all set out to look for the missing pie and loaf. Lina heard them coming, as well she might, for they were talking and quarrelling loud, and gave her master warning. They snatched up everything, and got all signs of their presence out at the back door before the servants entered. When they found nothing, they all turned on the chambermaid, and accused her, not only of lying against the pages, but of having taken the things herself. Their language and behaviour so disgusted Curdie, who could hear a great part of what passed, and he saw the danger of discovery now so much increased, that he began to devise how best at once to rid the palace of the whole pack of them. That, however, would be small gain so long as the treacherous officers of state continued in it. They must be first dealt with. A thought came to him, and the longer he looked at it the better he liked it.

As soon as the servants were gone, quarrelling and accusing all the way, they returned and finished their supper. Then Curdie, who had long been satisfied that Lina understood almost every word he said, communicated his plan to her, and knew by the wagging of her tail and the flashing of her eyes that she comprehended it. Until they had the king safe through the worst part of the night, however, nothing could be done.

They had now merely to go on waiting where they were till the household should be asleep. This waiting and waiting was much the hardest thing Curdie had to do in the whole affair. He took his mattock and, going again into the long passage, lighted a candle end and proceeded to examine the rock on all sides. But this was not merely to pass the time: he had a reason for it. When he broke the stone in the street, over which the baker fell, its appearance led him to pocket a fragment for further examination; and since then he had satisfied himself that it was the kind of stone in which gold is found, and that the yellow particles in it were pure metal. If such stone existed here in any plenty, he could soon make the king rich and independent of his ill-conditioned subjects. He was therefore now bent on an examination of the rock; nor had he been at it long before he was persuaded that there were large quantities of gold in the half-crystalline white stone, with its veins of opaque white and of green, of which the rock, so far as he had been able to inspect it, seemed almost entirely to consist. Every piece he broke was spotted with particles and little lumps of a lovely greenish yellow – and that was gold. Hitherto he had worked only in silver, but he had read, and heard talk, and knew, therefore, about gold. As soon as he had got the king free of rogues and villains, he would have all the best and most honest miners, with his father at the head of them, to work this rock for the king.

It was a great delight to him to use his mattock once more. The time went quickly, and when he left the passage to go to the king's chamber, he had already a good heap of fragments behind the broken door.

CHAPTER TWENTY-THREE

Dr Kelman

As soon as he had reason to hope the way was clear, Curdie ventured softly into the hall, with Lina behind him. There was no one asleep on the bench or floor, but by the fading fire sat a girl weeping. It was the same who had seen him carrying off the food, and had been so hardly used for saying so. She opened her eyes when he appeared, but did not seem frightened at him.

'I know why you weep,' said Curdie, 'and I am sorry for you.'

'It *is* hard not to be believed just *because* one speaks the truth,' said the girl, 'but that seems reason enough with some people. My mother taught me to speak the truth, and took such pains with me that I should find it hard to tell a lie, though I could invent many a story these servants would believe at once; for the truth is a strange thing here, and they don't know it when they see it. Show it them, and they all stare as if it were a wicked lie, and that with the lie yet warm that has just left their own mouths! You are a stranger,' she said, and burst out weeping afresh, 'but the stranger you are to such a place and such people the better!'

'I am the person,' said Curdie, 'whom you saw carrying the

things from the supper table.' He showed her the loaf. 'If you can trust, as well as speak the truth, I will trust you. Can you trust me?'

She looked at him steadily for a moment.

'I can,' she answered.

'One thing more,' said Curdie: 'have you courage as well as faith?'

'I think so.'

'Look my dog in the face and don't cry out. Come here, Lina.'

Lina obeyed. The girl looked at her, and laid her hand on Lina's head.

'Now I know you are a true woman,' said Curdie. 'I am come to set things right in this house. Not one of the servants knows I am here. Will you tell them tomorrow morning that, if they do not alter their ways, and give over drinking, and lying, and stealing, and unkindness, they shall every one of them be driven from the palace?'

'They will not believe me.'

'Most likely; but will you give them the chance?'

'I will.'

'Then I will be your friend. Wait here till I come again.'

She looked him once more in the face, and sat down.

When he reached the royal chamber, he found His Majesty awake, and very anxiously expecting him. He received him with the utmost kindness, and at once, as it were, put himself in his hands by telling him all he knew concerning the state he was in. His voice was feeble, but his eye was clear, although now and then his words and thoughts seemed to wander, Curdie could not be certain that the cause of their not being intelligible to him did not lie in himself. The king told him that for some years, ever since his queen's death, he had been losing heart over the wickedness of his people. He had tried hard to make them good, but they got worse and worse. Evil teachers, unknown to him, had crept into the schools; there was a general decay of truth and right principle at least in the city; and as that set the example to the nation, it must spread.

The main cause of his illness was the despondency with which the degeneration of his people affected him. He could not sleep, and had terrible dreams; while, to his unspeakable shame and distress, he doubted almost everybody. He had striven against his suspicion, but in vain, and his heart was sore, for his courtiers and councillors were really kind; only he could not think why none of their ladies came near his princess. The whole country was discontented, he heard, and there were signs of gathering storm outside as well as inside his borders. The master of the horse gave him sad news of the insubordination of the army; and his great white horse was dead, they told him; and his sword had lost its temper: it bent double the last time he tried it! — only perhaps that was in a dream; and they could not find his shield; and one of his spurs had lost the rowel.

Thus the poor king went wandering in a maze of sorrows, some of which were purely imaginary, while others were truer than he understood. He told how thieves came at night and tried to take his crown, so that he never dared let it out of his hands even when he slept; and how, every night, an evil demon in the shape of his physician came and poured poison down his throat. He knew it to be poison, he said, somehow, although it tasted like wine.

Here he stopped, faint with the unusual exertion of talking.

Curdie seized the flagon, and ran to the wine cellar.

In the servants' hall the girl still sat by the fire, waiting for him. As he returned he told her to follow him, and left her at the chamber door until he should rejoin her. When the king had had a little wine, he informed him that he had already discovered certain of His Majesty's enemies, and one of the worst of them was the doctor, for it was no other demon than the doctor himself who had been coming every night, and giving him a slow poison.

'So!' said the king. 'Then I have not been suspicious enough, for I thought it was but a dream! Is it possible Kelman can be such a wretch? Who then am I to trust?'

'Not one in the house, except the princess and myself,' said Curdie.

'I will not go to sleep,' said the king.

'That would be as bad as taking the poison,' said Curdie. 'No, no, sire; you must show your confidence by leaving all the watching to me, and doing all the sleeping Your Majesty can.'

The king smiled a contented smile, turned on his side, and was presently fast asleep. Then Curdie persuaded the princess also to go to sleep, and telling Lina to watch, went to the housemaid. He asked her if she could inform him which of the council slept in the palace, and show him their rooms. She knew every one of them, she said, and took him the round of all their doors, telling him which slept in each room. He then dismissed her, and returning to the king's chamber, seated himself behind a curtain at the head of the bed, on the side farthest from the king. He told Lina to get under the bed, and make no noise.

About one o'clock the doctor came stealing in. He looked

round for the princess, and seeing no one, smiled with satisfaction as he approached the wine where it stood under the lamp. Having partly filled a glass, he took from his pocket a small phial, and filled up the glass from it. The light fell upon his face from above, and Curdie saw the snake in it plainly visible. He had never beheld such an evil countenance: the man hated the king, and delighted in doing him wrong.

With the glass in his hand, he drew near the bed, set it down, and began his usual rude rousing of His Majesty. Not at once succeeding, he took a lancet from his pocket, and was parting its cover with an involuntary hiss of hate between his closed teeth, when Curdie stooped and whispered to Lina. 'Take him by the leg, Lina.' She darted noiselessly upon him. With a face of horrible consternation, he gave his leg one tug to free it; the next instant Curdie heard the one scrunch with which she crushed the bone like a stick of celery. He tumbled on the floor with a yell.

'Drag him out, Lina,' said Curdie.

Lina took him by the collar, and dragged him out. Her master followed her to direct her, and they left the doctor lying across the lord chamberlain's door, where he gave another horrible yell, and fainted.

The king had waked at his first cry, and by the time Curdie re-entered he had got at his sword where it hung from the centre of the tester, had drawn it, and was trying to get out of bed. But when Curdie told him all was well, he lay down again as quietly as a child comforted by his mother from a troubled dream. Curdie went to the door to watch.

The doctor's yells had aroused many, but not one had yet ventured to appear. Bells were rung violently, but none were answered; and in a minute or two Curdie had what he was watching for. The door of the lord chamberlain's room opened, and, pale with hideous terror, His Lordship peeped out. Seeing no one, he advanced to step into the corridor, and tumbled over the doctor. Curdie ran up, and held out his hand. He received in it the claw of a bird of prey – vulture or eagle, he could not tell which.

His Lordship, as soon as he was on his legs, taking him for one of the pages abused him heartily for not coming sooner, and threatened him with dismissal from the king's service for cowardice and neglect. He began indeed what bade fair to be a sermon on the duties of a page, but catching sight of the man who lay at his door, and seeing it was the doctor, he fell upon Curdie afresh for standing there doing nothing, and ordered him to fetch immediate assistance. Curdie left him, but slipped into the King's chamber, closed and locked the door, and left the rascals to look after each other. Ere long he heard hurrying footsteps, and for a few minutes there was a great muffled tumult of scuffling feet, low voices and deep groanings; then all was still again.

Irene slept through the whole – so confidently did she rest, knowing Curdie was in her father's room watching over him.

CHAPTER TWENTY-FOUR

The Prophecy

CURDIE sat and watched every motion of the sleeping king. All the night, to his ear, the palace lay as quiet as a nursery of healthful children. At sunrise he called the princess.

'How has His Majesty slept?' were her first words as she entered the room.

'Quite quietly,' answered Curdie; 'that is, since the doctor was got rid of.'

'How did you manage that?' inquired Irene; and Curdie had to tell all about it.

'How terrible!' she said. 'Did it not startle the king dreadfully?'

'It did rather. I found him getting out of bed, sword in hand.'

'The brave old man!' cried the princess.

'Not so old!' said Curdie, 'as you will soon see. He went off again in a minute or so; but for a little while he was restless, and once when he lifted his hand it came down on the spikes of his crown, and he half waked.'

'But where *is* the crown?' cried Irene, in sudden terror.

'I stroked his hands,' answered Curdie, 'and took the crown from them; and ever since he has slept quietly, and again and again smiled in his sleep.'

'I have never seen him do that,' said the princess. 'But what have you done with the crown, Curdie?'

'Look,' said Curdie, moving away from the bedside.

Irene followed him – and there, in the middle of the floor, she saw a strange sight. Lina lay at full length, fast asleep, her tail stretched out straight behind her and her forelegs before her: between the two paws meeting in front of it, her nose just touching it behind, glowed and flashed the crown, like a nest of the humming birds of heaven.

Irene gazed, and looked up with a smile.

'But what if the thief were to come, and she not to wake?' she said. 'Shall I try her?' And as she spoke she stopped toward the crown.

'No, no, no!' cried Curdie, terrified. 'She would frighten you out of your wits. I would do it to show you, but she would wake your father. You have no conception with what a roar she would spring at my throat. But you shall see how lightly she wakes the moment I speak to her. Lina!'

She was on her feet ·the same instant, with her great tail sticking out straight behind her, just as it had been lying.

'Good dog!' said the princess, and patted her head. Lina wagged her tail solemnly, like the boom of an anchored sloop. Irene took the crown, and laid it where the king would see it when he woke.

'Now, Princess,' said Curdie, 'I must leave you for a few minutes. You must bolt the door, please, and not open it to any one.'

Away to the cellar he went with Lina, taking care, as they passed through the servants' hall, to get her a good breakfast. In about one minute she had eaten what he gave her, and looked up in his face: it was not more she wanted, but work. So out of the cellar they went through the passage, and Curdie into the dungeon, where he pulled up Lina, opened the door, let her out, and shut it again behind her. As he reached the door of the king's chamber, Lina was flying out of the gate of Gwyntystorm as fast as her mighty legs could carry her.

'What's come to the wench?' growled the menservants one to another, when the chambermaid appeared among them the next morning. There was something in her face which they could not understand, and did not like.

'Are we all dirt?' they said. 'What are you thinking about? Have you seen yourself in the glass this morning, miss?'

She made no answer.

'Do you want to be treated as you deserve, or will you speak, you hussy?' said the first woman-cook. 'I would fain know what right *you* have to put on a face like that!'

'You won't believe me,' said the girl.

'Of course not. What is it?'

'I must tell you, whether you believe me or not,' she said.

'Of course you must.'

'It is this, then: if you do not repent of your bad ways, you are all going to be punished — all turned out of the palace together.'

'A mighty punishment!' said the butler. 'A good riddance, say I, of the trouble of keeping minxes like you in order! And why, pray, should we be turned out? What have I to repent of now, your holiness?'

'That you know best yourself,' said the girl.

'A pretty piece of insolence! How should *I* know, forsooth, what a menial like you has got against me! There *are* people in this house — oh! I'm not blind to their ways! — but everyone for himself, say I! Pray, Miss Judgement, who gave you such an impertinent message to His Majesty's household?'

'One who is come to set things right in the king's house.'

'Right, indeed!' cried the butler: but that moment the thought came back to him of the roar he had heard in the cellar, and he turned pale and was silent.

The steward took it up next.

'And pray, pretty prophetess,' he said, attempting to chuck her under the chin, 'what have *I* got to repent of?'

'That you know best yourself,' said the girl. 'You have but to look into your books or your heart.'

'Can you tell *me*, then, what I have to repent of?' said the groom of the chambers.

'That you know best yourself,' said the girl once more. 'The person who told me to tell you said the servants of this house had to repent of thieving, and lying, and unkindness, and drinking; and they will be made to repent of them one way, if they don't do it of themselves another.'

Then arose a great hubbub; for by this time all the servants in the house were gathered about her, and all talked together, in towering indignation.

'Thieving, indeed!' cried one. 'A pretty word in a house where everything is left lying about in a shameless way, tempting poor innocent girls! A house where nobody cares for anything, or has the least respect to the value of property!'

'I suppose you envy me this brooch of mine,' said another. 'There was just a half sheet of note paper about it, not a scrap more, in a drawer that's always open in the writing table in the study! What sort of place is that for a jewel? Can you call it stealing to take a thing from such a place as that? Nobody cared a straw about it. It might as well have been in the dust hole! If it had been locked up — then, to be sure!'

'Drinking!' said the chief porter, with a husky laugh. 'And who wouldn't drink when he had a chance? Or who would repent it, except that the drink was gone? Tell me that, Miss Innocence.'

'Lying!' said a great, coarse footman. 'I suppose you mean when I told you yesterday you were a pretty girl when you didn't pout? Lying, indeed! Tell us something worth repenting of! Lying is the way of Gwyntystorm. You should have heard Jabez lying to the cook last night! He wanted a sweetbread for his pup, and pretended it was for the princess! Ha! ha! ha!'

'Unkindness! I wonder who's unkind! Going and listening to any stranger against her fellow servants, and then bringing back his wicked words to trouble them!' said the oldest and worst of the housemaids. 'One of ourselves, too! Come, you hypocrite! This is all an invention of yours and your young man's, to take your revenge of us because we found you out in a lie last night. Tell true now: wasn't it the same that stole the loaf and the pie that sent you with the impudent message?'

As she said this, she stepped up to the housemaid and gave her, instead of time to answer, a box on the ear that almost threw her down; and whoever could get at her began to push and bustle and pinch and punch her.

'You invite your fate,' she said quietly.

They fell furiously upon her, drove her from the hall with kicks and blows, hustled her along the passage, and threw her down the stair to the wine cellar, then locked the door at the top of it, and went back to their breakfast.

In the meantime the king and the princess had had their bread and wine, and the princess, with Curdie's help, had

155

made the room as tidy as she could — they were terribly neglected by the servants. And now Curdie set himself to interest and amuse the king, and prevent him from thinking too much, in order that he might the sooner think the better. Presently, at His Majesty's request, he began from the beginning, and told everything he could recall of his life, about his father and mother and their cottage on the mountain, of the inside of the mountain and the work there, about the goblins and his adventures with them.

When he came to finding the princess and her nurse overtaken by the twilight on the mountain, Irene took up her share of the tale, and told all about herself to that point, and then Curdie took it up again; and so they went on, each fitting in the part that the other did not know, thus keeping the hoop of the story running straight; and the king listened with wondering and delighted ears, astonished to find what he could so ill comprehend, yet fitting so well together from the lips of two narrators.

At last, with the mission given him by the wonderful princess and his consequent adventures, Curdie brought up the whole tale to the present moment. Then a silence fell, and Irene and Curdie thought the king was asleep. But he was far from it; he was thinking about many things. After a long pause he said:

'Now at last, my children, I am compelled to believe many things I could not and do not yet understand — things I used to hear, and sometimes see, as often as I visited my mother's home. Once, for instance, I heard my mother say to her father — speaking of me — "He is a good, honest boy, but he will be an old man before he understands"; and my grandfather answered, "Keep up your heart, child: my mother will look after him." I thought often of their words, and the many strange things besides I both heard and saw in that house: but by degrees, because I could not understand them, I gave up thinking of them. And indeed I had almost forgotten them, when you, my child, talking that day about the Queen Irene and her pigeons, and what you had seen in her garret, brought them all back to my mind in a vague mass. But now they keep coming back to me, one by one, every one for itself; and I shall just hold my peace, and lie here quite still, and think about them all till I get well again.'

What he meant they could not quite understand, but they saw plainly that already he was better.

'Put away my crown,' he said. 'I am tired of seeing it, and have no more any fear of its safety.'

They put it away together, withdrew from the bedside, and left him in peace.

CHAPTER TWENTY-FIVE

The Avengers

THERE was nothing now to be dreaded from Dr Kelman, but it made Curdie anxious, as the evening drew near, to think that not a soul belonging to the court had been to visit the king, or ask how he did, that day. He feared, in some shape or other, a more determined assault. He had provided himself a place in the room, to which he might retreat upon approach, and whence he could watch; but not once had he had to betake himself to it.

Towards night the king fell asleep. Curdie thought more and more uneasily of the moment when he must again leave them for a little while. Deeper and deeper fell the shadows. No one came to light the lamp. The princess drew her chair close to Curdie: she would rather it were not so dark, she said. She was afraid of something – she could not tell what; nor could she give any reason for her fear, but that all was so dreadfully still.

When it had been dark about an hour, Curdie thought Lina might have returned; and reflected that the sooner he went the less danger was there of any assault while he was away. There was more risk of his own presence being discovered, no doubt, but things were now drawing to a crisis, and it must be run. So, telling the princess to lock all the doors of the bedchamber, and let no one in, he took his mattock, and with here a run, and there a halt under cover, gained the door at the head of the cellar stair in safety. To his surprise he found it locked, and the key was gone. There was no time for deliberation. He felt where the lock was, and dealt it a tremendous blow with his mattock. It needed but a second to dash the door open. Someone laid a hand on his arm.

'Who is it?' said Curdie.

'I told you they wouldn't believe me, sir,' said the housemaid. 'I have been here all day.'

He took her hand, and said, 'You are a good, brave girl. Now come with me, lest your enemies imprison you again.'

He took her to the cellar, locked the door, lighted a bit of candle, gave her a little wine, told her to wait there till he came, and went out the back way.

Swiftly he swung himself up into the dungeon. Lina had done her part. The place was swarming with creatures — animal forms wilder and more grotesque than ever ramped in nightmare dream. Close by the hole, waiting his coming, her green eyes piercing the gulf below, Lina had but just laid herself down when he appeared. All about the vault and up the slope of the rubbish heap lay and stood and squatted the forty-nine whose friendship Lina had conquered in the wood. They all came crowding about Curdie.

He must get them into the cellar as quickly as ever he could. But when he looked at the size of some of them, he feared it would be a long business to enlarge the hole sufficiently to let them through. At it he rushed, hitting vigorously at the edge with his mattock. At the very first blow came a splash from the water beneath, but ere he could heave a third, a creature like a tapir, only that the grasping point of its proboscis was hard as the steel of Curdie's hammer, pushed him gently aside, making room for another creature, with a head like a great club, which it began banging upon the floor with terrible force and noise. After about a minute of this battery, the tapir came up again, shoved Clubhead aside, and putting its own head into the hole began gnawing at the sides of it with the finger of its nose, in such a fashion that the fragments fell in a continuous gravelly shower into the water. In a few minutes the opening was large enough for the biggest creature among them to get through it.

Next came the difficulty of letting them down: some were quite light, but the half of them were too heavy for the rope, not to say for his arms. The creatures themselves seemed to be puzzling where or how they were to go. One after another of them came up, looked down through the hole, and drew back. Curdie thought if he let Lina down, perhaps that would suggest something; possibly they did not see the opening on the other side. He did so, and Lina stood lighting up the entrance of the passage with her gleaming eyes.

One by one the creatures looked down again, and one by one they drew back, each standing aside to glance at the next, as if to say, *Now you have a look.* At last it came to the turn of the serpent with the long body, the four short legs behind, and the little wings before. No sooner had he poked his head through than he poked it farther through – and farther, and farther yet, until there was little more than his legs left in the dungeon. By that time he had got his head and neck well into the passage beside Lina. Then his legs gave a great waddle and spring, and he tumbled himself, far as there was betwixt them, heels over head into the passage.

'That is all very well for you, Mr Legserpent!' thought Curdie to himself; 'but what is to be done with the rest?'

He had hardly time to think it, however, before the creature's head appeared again through the floor. He caught hold of the bar of iron to which Curdie's rope was tied, and settling it securely across the narrowest part of the irregular opening, held fast to it with his teeth. It was plain to Curdie, from the universal hardness among them, that they must all, at one time or another, have been creatures of the mines.

He saw at once what this one was after. The beast had planted his feet firmly upon the floor of the passage, and stretched his long body up and across the chasm to serve as a bridge for the rest. Curdie mounted instantly upon his neck, threw his arms round him as far as they would go, and slid down in ease and safety, the bridge just bending a little as his weight glided over it. But he thought some of the creatures would try the legserpent's teeth.

One by one the oddities followed, and slid down in safety. When they seemed to be all landed, he counted them: there were but forty-eight. Up the rope again he went, and found one which had been afraid to trust himself to the bridge, and no wonder! for he had neither legs nor head nor arms nor tail: he was just a round thing, about a foot in diameter, with a nose and mouth and eyes on one side of the ball. He had made his journey by rolling as swiftly as the fleetest of them could run. The back of the legserpent not being flat, he could not quite trust himself to roll straight and not drop into the gulf. Curdie took him in his arms, and the moment he looked down through the hole, the bridge made itself again, and he slid into the passage in safety, with Ballbody in his bosom.

He ran first to the cellar to warn the girl not to be frightened

161

at the avengers of wickedness. Then he called to Lina to bring in her friends.

One after another they came trooping in, till the cellar seemed full of them. The housemaid regarded them without fear.

'Sir,' she said, 'there is one of the pages I don't take to be a bad fellow.'

'Then keep him near you,' said Curdie. 'And now can you show me a way to the king's chamber not through the servants' hall?'

'There is a way through the chamber of the colonel of the guard,' she answered, 'but he is ill, and in bed.'

'Take me that way,' said Curdie.

By many ups and downs and windings and turnings she brought him to a dimly lighted room, where lay an elderly man asleep. His arm was outside the coverlid, and Curdie gave his hand a hurried grasp as he went by. His heart beat for joy, for he had found a good, honest, human hand.

'I suppose that is why he is ill,' he said to himself.

It was now close upon suppertime, and when the girl stopped at the door of the king's chamber, he told her to go and give the servants one warning more.

'Say the messenger sent you,' he said. 'I will be with you very soon.'

The king was still asleep. Curdie talked to the princess for a few minutes, told her not to be frightened whatever noises she heard, only to keep her door locked till he came, and left her.

CHAPTER TWENTY-SIX

The Vengeance

By the time the girl reached the servants' hall they were seated at supper. A loud, confused exclamation arose when she entered. No one made room for her; all stared with unfriendly eyes. A page, who entered the next minute by another door, came to her side.

'Where do *you* come from, hussy?' shouted the butler, and knocked his fist on the table with a loud clang.

He had gone to fetch wine, had found the stair door broken open and the cellar door locked, and had turned and fled. Among his fellows, however, he had now regained what courage could be called his.

'From the cellar,' she replied. 'The messenger broke open the door, and sent me to you again.'

'The messenger! Pooh! What messenger?'

'The same who sent me before to tell you to repent.'

'What! Will you go fooling it still? Haven't you had enough of it?' cried the butler in a rage, and starting to his feet, drew near threateningly.

'I must do as I am told,' said the girl.

'Then why *don't* you do as *I* tell you, and hold your tongue?' said the butler. 'Who wants your preachments? If anybody here has anything to repent of, isn't that enough — and more than enough for him — but you must come bothering about, and stirring up, till not a drop of quiet will settle inside him? You come along with me, young woman; we'll see if we can't find a lock somewhere in the house that'll hold you in!'

'Hands off, Mr. Butler!' said the page, and stepped between between.

'Oh, ho!' cried the butler, and pointed his fat finger at him. 'That's you, is it, my fine fellow? So it's you that's up to her tricks, is it?'

The youth did not answer, only stood with flashing eyes fixed on him, until, growing angrier and angrier, but not daring a step nearer, he burst out with a rude but quavering authority:

'Leave the house, both of you! Be off, or I'll have Mr Steward to talk to you. Threaten your masters, indeed! Out of the house with you, and show us the way you tell us of!'

Two or three of the footmen got up and ranged themselves behind the butler.

'Don't say I threaten you, Mr Butler,' expostulated the girl from behind the page. 'The messenger said I was to tell you again, and give you one chance more.'

'Did the *messenger* mention me in particular?' asked the butler, looking the page unsteadily in the face.

'No, sir,' answered the girl.

'I thought not! I should like to hear him!'

'Then hear him now,' said Curdie, who that moment entered at the opposite corner of the hall. 'I speak of the butler in particular when I say that I know more evil of him than of any of the rest. He will not let either his own conscience or my messenger speak to him: I therefore now speak myself. I proclaim him a villain, and a traitor to His Majesty the king. But what better is any one of you who cares only for himself, eats, drinks, takes good money, and gives vile service in return, stealing and wasting the king's property, and making of the palace, which ought to be an example of order and sobriety, a disgrace to the country?'

For a moment all stood astonished into silence by this bold speech from a stranger. True, they saw by his mattock over his shoulder that he was nothing but a miner boy yet for a moment the truth told notwithstanding. Then a great roaring laugh burst from the biggest of the footmen as he came shouldering his way through the crowd toward Curdie.

'Yes, I'm right,' he cried; 'I thought as much! This *messenger*, forsooth, is nothing but a gallows bird — a fellow the city marshal was going to hang, but unfortunately put it off till he should be starved enough to save rope and be throttled with a pack thread. He broke prison, and here he is preaching!'

As he spoke, he stretched out his great hand to lay hold of him. Curdie caught it in his left hand, and heaved his mattock with the other. Finding, however, nothing worse than an ox hoof, he restrained himself, stepped back a pace or two, shifted his mattock to his left hand, and struck him a little smart blow on the shoulder. His arm dropped by his side, he gave a roar, and drew back.

His fellows came crowding upon Curdie. Some called to the dogs; others swore; the women screamed; the footmen and pages got round him in a half circle, which he kept from closing by swinging his mattock, and here and there threatening a blow.

'Whoever confesses to having done anything wrong in this house, however small, however great, and means to do better, let him come to this corner of the room,' he cried.

None moved but the page, who went toward him skirting the wall. When they caught sight of him, the crowd broke into a hiss of derision.

'There! See! Look at the sinner! He confesses! Actually confesses! Come, what is it you stole? The barefaced hypocrite! There's your sort to set up for reproving other people! Where's the other now?'

But the maid had left the room, and they let the page pass, for he looked dangerous to stop. Curdie had just put him betwixt him and the wall, behind the door, when in rushed the butler with the huge kitchen poker, the point of which he had blown red-hot in the fire, followed by the cook with his longest spit. Through the crowd, which scattered right and left before them, they came down upon Curdie. Uttering a shrill whistle, he caught the poker a blow with his mattock, knocking the point to the ground, while the page behind him started forward, and seizing the point of the spit, held on to it with both hands, the cook kicking him furiously.

Ere the butler could raise the poker again, or the cook recover the spit, with a roar to terrify the dead, Lina dashed into the room, her eyes flaming like candles. She went straight at the butler. He was down in a moment, and she on the top of him, wagging her tail over him like a lioness.

'Don't kill him, Lina,' said Curdie.

'Oh, Mr Miner!' cried the butler.

'Put your foot on his mouth, Lina,' said Curdie. 'The truth Fear tells is not much better than her lies.'

The rest of the creatures now came stalking, rolling,

leaping, gliding, hobbling into the room, and each as he came took the next place along the wall, until, solemn and grotesque, all stood ranged, awaiting orders.

And now some of the culprits were stealing to the doors nearest them. Curdie whispered to the two creatures next him. Off went Ballbody, rolling and bounding through the crowd like a spent cannon shot, and when the foremost reached the door to the corridor, there he lay at the foot of it grinning; to the other door scuttled a scorpion, as big as a huge crab. The rest stood so still that some began to think they were only boys dressed up to look awful; they persuaded themselves they were only another part of the housemaid's and page's vengeful contrivance, and their evil spirits began to rise again. Meantime Curdie had, with a second sharp blow from the hammer of his mattock, disabled the cook, so that he yielded the spit with a groan. He now turned to the avengers.

'Go at them,' he said.

The whole nine-and-forty obeyed at once, each for himself, and after his own fashion. A scene of confusion and terror followed. The crowd scattered like a dance of flies. The creatures had been instructed not to hurt much, but to hunt incessantly, until everyone had rushed from the house. The women shrieked, and ran hither and thither through the hall, pursued each by her own horror, and snapped at by every other in passing. If one threw herself down in hysterical despair, she was instantly poked or clawed or nibbled up again.

Though they were quite as frightened at first, the men did not run so fast; and by and by some of them finding they were only glared at, and followed, and pushed, began to summon up courage once more, and with courage came impudence.

The tapir had the big footman in charge: the fellow stood stock-still, and let the beast come up to him, then put out his finger and playfully patted his nose. The tapir gave the nose a little twist, and the finger lay on the floor. Then indeed did the footman run.

Gradually the avengers grew more severe, and the terrors of the imagination were fast yielding to those of sensuous experience, when a page, perceiving one of the doors no longer guarded, sprang at it, and ran out. Another and another followed. Not a beast went after, until, one by one, they were every one gone from the hall, and the whole crew in the kitchen.

There they were beginning to congratulate themselves that all was over, when in came the creatures trooping after them, and the second act of their terror and pain began. They were flung about in all directions; their clothes were torn from them; they were pinched and scratched any – and every-where; Ballbody kept rolling up them and over them, confining his attentions to no one in particular; the scorpion kept grabbing at their legs with his huge pincers; a three-foot centipede kept screwing up their bodies, nipping as he went; varied as numerous were their woes. Nor was it long before the last of them had fled from the kitchen to the sculleries.

But thither also they were followed, and there again they were hunted about. They were bespattered with the dirt of their own neglect; they were soused in the stinking water that had boiled greens; they were smeared with rancid dripping; their faces were rubbed in maggots: I dare not tell all that was done to them. At last they got the door into a back yard open, and rushed out. Then first they knew that the wind was howling and the rain falling in sheets. But there was no rest for them even there. Thither also were they followed by the inexorable avengers, and the only door here was a door out of the palace: out every soul of them was driven, and left, some standing, some lying, some crawling, to the farther buffeting of the waterspouts and whirlwinds ranging every street of the city. The door was flung to behind them, and they heard it locked and bolted and barred against them.

CHAPTER TWENTY-SEVEN

More Vengeance

As soon as they were gone, Curdie brought the creatures back to the servants' hall, and told them to eat up everything on the table. It *was* a sight to see them all standing round it — except such as had to get upon it — eating and drinking, each after its fashion, without a smile, or a word, or a glance of fellowship in the act. A very few moments served to make everything eatable vanish, and then Curdie requested them to clean house, and the page who stood by to assist them.

Every one set about it except Ballbody: he could do nothing at cleaning, for the more *he* rolled, the more he spread the dirt. Curdie was curious to know what he had been, and how he had come to be such as he was: but he could only conjecture that he was a gluttonous alderman whom nature had treated homeopathically.

And now there was such a cleaning and clearing out of neglected places, such a burying and burning of refuse, such a rinsing of jugs, such a swilling of sinks, and such a flushing of drains as would have delighted the eyes of all true housekeepers and lovers of cleanliness generally.

Curdie meantime was with the king, telling him all he had done. They had heard a little noise, but not much, for he had old the avengers to repress outcry as much as possible; and they had seen to it that the more anyone cried out the more he had to cry out upon, while the patient ones they scarcely hurt at all.

Having promised His Majesty and Her Royal Highness a good breakfast, Curdie now went to finish the business. The courtiers must be dealt with. A few who were the worst, and the leaders of the rest, must be made examples of; the others should be driven to the street.

He found the chiefs of the conspiracy holding a final consultation in the smaller room off the hall. These were the lord chamberlain, the attorney-general, the master of the horse, and the king's private secretary: the lord chancellor and the rest, as foolish as faithless, were but the tools of these.

The housemaid had shown him a little closet, opening from a passage behind, where he could overhear all that passed in that room; and now Curdie heard enough to understand that they had determined, in the dead of that night, rather in the deepest dark before the morning, to bring a certain company of soldiers into the palace, make away with the king, secure the princess, announce the sudden death of His Majesty, read as his the will they had drawn up, and proceed to govern the country at their ease, and with results: they would at once levy severer taxes, and pick a quarrel with the most powerful of their neighbours. Everything settled, they agreed to retire, and have a few hours' quiet sleep first – all but the secretary, who was to sit up and call them at the proper moment. Curdie allowed them half an hour to get to bed, and then set about completing his purgation of the palace.

First he called Lina, and opened the door of the room where the secretary sat. She crept in, and laid herself down against it.

When the secretary, rising to stretch his legs, caught sight of her eyes, he stood frozen with terror. She made neither motion nor sound. Gathering courage, and taking the thing for a spectral illusion, he made a step forward. She showed her other teeth, with a growl neither more than audible nor less than horrible. The secretary sank fainting into a chair. He was not a brave man, and besides, his conscience had gone over to the enemy, and was sitting against the door by Lina.

To the lord chamberlain's door next, Curdie conducted the legserpent, and let him in.

Now His Lordship had had a bedstead made for himself, sweetly fashioned of rods of silver gilt: upon it the legserpent found him asleep, and under it he crept. But out he came on the other side, and crept over it next, and again under it, and so over it, under it, over it, five or six times, every time leaving a coil of himself behind him, until he had softly folded all his length about the lord chamberlain and his bed. This done, he set up his head, looking down with curved neck right over His Lordship's, and began to hiss in his face.

He woke in terror unspeakable, and would have started up, but the moment he moved, the legserpent drew his coil closer, and closer still, and drew and drew until the quaking traitor heard the joints of his bedstead grinding and gnarring. Presently he persuaded himself that it was only a horrid nightmare, and began to struggle with all his strength to throw it off. Thereupon the legserpent gave his hooked nose such a bite that his teeth met through it — but it was hardly thicker than the bowl of a spoon; and then the vulture knew that he was in the grasp of his enemy the snake, and yielded.

As soon as he was quiet the legserpent began to untwist and retwist, to uncoil and recoil himself, swinging and swaying knotting and relaxing himself with strangest curves and convolutions, always, however, leaving at least one coil around his victim. At last he undid himself entirely, and crept from the bed. Then first the lord chamberlain discovered that his tormentor had bent and twisted the bedstead, legs and canopy and all, so about him that he was shut in a silver cage out of which it was impossible for him to find a way. Once more, thinking his enemy was gone, he began to shout for help. But the instant he opened his mouth his keeper darted at him and bit him, and after three or four such essays, he lay still.

The master of the horse Curdie gave in charge to the tapir. When the soldier saw him enter — for he was not yet asleep — he sprang from his bed, and flew at him with his sword. But the creature's hide was invulnerable to his blows, and he pecked at his legs with his proboscis until he jumped into bed again, groaning, and covered himself up; after which the tapir contented himself with now and then paying a visit to his toes.

As for the attorney-general, Curdie led to his door a huge spider, about two feet long in the body, which, having made an excellent supper, was full of webbing. The attorney-general had not gone to bed, but sat in a chair asleep before a great mirror. He had been trying the effect of a diamond star which he had that morning taken from the jewel room. When he woke he fancied himself paralysed; every limb, every finger even, was motionless: coils and coils of broad spider ribbon bandaged his members to his body, and all to the chair. In the glass he saw himself wound about with slavery infinite. On a footstool a yard off sat the spider glaring at him.

Clubhead had mounted guard over the butler, where he lay tied hand and foot under the third cask. From that cask he had seen the wine run into a great bath, and therein he expected to be drowned. The doctor, with his crushed leg, needed no one to guard him.

And now Curdie proceeded to the expulsion of the rest. Great men or underlings, he treated them all alike. From room to room over the house he went, and sleeping or waking took the man by the hand. Such was the state to which a year of wicked rule had reduced the moral condition of the court, that in it all he found but three with human hands. The possessors of these he allowed to dress themselves and depart in peace. When they perceived his mission, and how he was backed, they yielded.

Then commenced a general hunt, to clear the house of the vermin. Out of their beds in their night clothing, out of their rooms, gorgeous chambers or garret nooks, the creatures hunted them. Not one was allowed to escape. Tumult and noise there was little, for fear was too deadly for outcry. Ferreting them out everywhere, following them upstairs and downstairs, yielding no instant of repose except upon the way out, the avengers persecuted the miscreants, until the last of them was shivering outside the palace gates, with hardly sense enough left to know where to run.

When they set out to look for shelter, they found every inn full of the servants expelled before them, and not one would yield his place to a superior suddenly levelled with himself. Most houses refused to admit them on the ground of the wickedness that must have drawn on them such a punishment; and not a few would have been left in the streets all night, had not Derba, roused by the vain entreaties at the doors on each side of her cottage, opened hers, and given up everything to them. The lord chancellor was only too glad to share a mattress with a stableboy, and steal his bare feet under his jacket.

In the morning Curdie appeared, and the outcasts were in terror, thinking he had come after them again. But he took no notice of them: his object was to request Derba to go to the palace: the king required her services. She need take no trouble about her cottage, he said; the palace was henceforward her home: she was the king's chatelaine over men and maidens of his household. And this very morning she must cook His Majesty a nice breakfast.

CHAPTER TWENTY-EIGHT

The Preacher

VARIOUS reports went undulating through the city as to the nature of what had taken place in the palace. The people gathered, and stared at the house, eyeing it as if it had sprung up in the night. But it looked sedate enough, remaining closed and silent, like a house that was dead. They saw no one come out or go in. Smoke arose from a chimney or two; there was hardly another sign of life. It was not for some little time generally understood that the highest officers of the crown as well as the lowest menials of the palace had been dismissed in disgrace: for who was to recognize a lord chancellor in his nightshirt? And what lord chancellor would, so attired in the street, proclaim his rank and office aloud? Before it was day most of the courtiers crept down to the river, hired boats, and betook themselves to their homes or their friends in the country. It was assumed in the city that the domestics had been discharged upon a sudden discovery of general and unpardonable peculation; for, almost everybody being guilty of it himself, petty dishonesty was the crime most easily credited and least easily passed over in Gwyntystorm.

Now that same day was Religion day, and not a few of the clergy, always glad to seize on any passing event to give interest to the dull and monotonic grind of their intellectual machines, made this remarkable one the ground of discourse to their congregations. More especially than the rest, the first priest of the great temple where was the royal pew, judged himself, from his relation to the palace, called upon to 'improve the occasion', for they talked ever about improvement at Gwyntystorm, all the time they were going down hill with a rush.

The book which had, of late years, come to be considered the most sacred, was called *The Book of Nations*, and consisted of proverbs, and history traced through custom: from it the first priest chose his text; and his text was, 'Honesty Is the Best Policy.' He was considered a very eloquent man, but I can offer only a few of the larger bones of his sermon.

The main proof of the verity of their religion, he said, was that things always went well with those who profess it; and its first fundamental principle, grounded in inborn invariable instinct, was, that every One should take care of that One. This was the first duty of Man. If every one would but obey this law, number one, then would every one be perfectly cared for – one being always equal to one. But the faculty of care was in excess of need, and all that overflowed, and would otherwise run to waste, ought to be gently turned in the direction of one's neighbour, seeing that this also wrought for the fulfilling of the law, inasmuch as the reaction of excess so directed was upon the director of the same, to the comfort, that is, and well-being of the original self. To be just and friendly was to build the warmest and safest of all nests, and to be kind and loving was to line it with the softest of all furs and feathers, for the one precious, comfort-loving self there to lie, revelling in downiest bliss. One of the laws therefore most

177

binding upon men because of its relation to the first and greatest of all duties, was embodied in the Proverb he had just read; and what stronger proof of its wisdom and truth could they desire than the sudden and complete vengeance which had fallen upon those worse than ordinary sinners who had offended against the king's majesty by forgetting that 'Honesty Is the Best Policy'?

At this point of the discourse the head of the legserpent rose from the floor of the temple, towering above the pulpit, above the priest, then curving downward, with open mouth slowly descended upon him. Horror froze the sermon-pump. He stared upward aghast. The great teeth of the animal closed upon a mouthful of the sacred vestments, and slowly he lifted the preacher from the pulpit, like a handful of linen from a washtub, and, on his four solemn stumps, bore him out of the temple, dangling aloft from his jaws. At the back of it he dropped him into the dust hole among the remnants of a library whose age had destroyed its value in the eyes of the chapter. They found him burrowing in it, a lunatic henceforth – whose madness presented the peculiar feature, that in its paroxysms he jabbered sense.

Bone-freezing horror pervaded Gwyntystorm. If their best and wisest were treated with such contempt, what might not the rest of them look for? Alas for their city! Their grandly respectable city! Their loftily reasonable city! Where it was all to end, who could tell!

But something must be done. Hastily assembling, the priests chose a new first priest, and in full conclave unanimously declared and accepted that the king in his retirement had, through the practice of the blackest magic, turned the palace into a nest of demons in the midst of them. A grand exorcism was therefore indispensable.

In the meantime the fact came out that the greater part of the courtiers had been dismissed as well as the servants, and this fact swelled the hope of the Party of Decency, as they called themselves. Upon it they proceeded to act, and strengthened themselves on all sides.

The action of the king's bodyguard remained for a time uncertain. But when at length its officers were satisfied that both the master of the horse and their colonel were missing, they placed themselves under the orders of the first priest.

Every one dated the culmination of the evil from the visit of the miner and his mongrel; and the butchers vowed, if they could but get hold of them again, they would roast both of them alive. At once they formed themselves into a regiment, and put their dogs in training for attack.

Incessant was the talk, innumerable were the suggestions, and great was the deliberation. The general consent, however, was that as soon as the priests should have expelled the demons, they would depose the king, and attired in all his regal insignia, shut him in a cage for public show; then choose governors, with the lord chancellor at their head, whose first duty should be to remit every possible tax; and the magistrates, by the mouth of the city marshal, required all able-bodied citizens, in order to do their part toward the carrying out of these and a multitude of other reforms, to be ready to take arms at the first summons.

Things needful were prepared as speedily as possible, and a mighty ceremony, in the temple, in the market place, and in front of the palace, was performed for the expulsion of the demons. This over, the leaders retired to arrange an attack upon the palace.

But that night events occurred which, proving the failure of their first, induced the abandonment of their second, intent. Certain of the prowling order of the community, whose numbers had of late been steadily on the increase, reported frightful things. Demons of indescribable ugliness had been espied careering through the midnight streets and courts. A citizen — some said in the very act of housebreaking, but no one cared to look into trifles at such a crisis — had been seized from behind, he could not see by what, and soused in the river. A well-known receiver of stolen goods had had his shop broken open, and when he came down in the morning had found everything in ruin on the pavement. The wooden image of justice over the door of the city marshal had had the arm that held the sword *bitten* off. The gluttonous magistrate had been pulled from his bed in the dark, by beings of which he could see nothing but the flaming eyes, and treated to a bath of the turtle soup that had been left simmering by the side of the kitchen fire. Having poured it over him, they put him again into his bed, where he soon learned how a mummy must feel in its cerements.

Worst of all, in the market place was fixed up a paper, with the king's own signature, to the effect that whoever henceforth should show inhospitality to strangers, and should be convicted of the same, should be instantly expelled the city; while a second, in the butchers' quarter, ordained that any dog which henceforth should attack a stranger should be immediately destroyed. It was plain, said the butchers, that the clergy were of no use; *they* could not exorcise demons! That afternoon, catching sight of a poor old fellow in rags and tatters, quietly walking up the street, they hounded their dogs upon him, and had it not been that the door of Derba's cottage was standing open, and was near enough for him to dart in and shut it ere they reached him, he would have been torn in pieces.

And thus things went on for some days.

CHAPTER TWENTY-NINE

Barbara

IN the meantime, with Derba to minister to his wants, with
Curdie to protect him, and Irene to nurse him, the king was
getting rapidly stronger. Good food was what he most
wanted and of that, at least of certain kinds of it, there was
plentiful store in the palace. Everywhere since the cleansing of
the lower regions of it, the air was clean and sweet, and under
the honest hands of the one housemaid the king's chamber
became a pleasure to his eyes. With such changes it was no
wonder if his heart grew lighter as well as his brain clearer.

But still evil dreams came and troubled him, the lingering
result of the wicked medicines the doctor had given him.
Every night, sometimes twice or thrice, he would wake up in
terror, and it would be minutes ere he could come to himself.
The consequence was that he was always worse in the morning, and had loss to make up during the day. While he slept,
Irene or Curdie, one or the other, must still be always by his
side.

One night, when it was Curdie's turn with the king, he
heard a cry somewhere in the house, and as there was no other
child, concluded, notwithstanding the distance of her
grandmother's room, that it must be Barbara. Fearing some-

thing might be wrong, and noting the king's sleep more quiet than usual, he ran to see. He found the child in the middle of the floor, weeping bitterly, and Derba slumbering peacefully in bed. The instant she saw him the night-lost thing ceased her crying, smiled, and stretched out her arms to him. Unwilling to wake the old woman, who had been working hard all day, he took the child, and carried her with him. She clung to him so, pressing her tear-wet radiant face against his, that her little arms threatened to choke him.

When he re-entered the chamber, he found the king sitting up in bed, fighting the phantoms of some hideous dream. Generally upon such occasions, although he saw his watcher, he could not dissociate him from the dream, and went raving on. But the moment his eyes fell upon little Barbara, whom he had never seen before, his soul came into them with a rush, and a smile like the dawn of an eternal day overspread his countenance; the dream was nowhere, and the child was in his heart. He stretched out his arms to her, the child stretched out hers to him, and in five minutes they were both asleep, each in the other's embrace.

From that night Barbara had a crib in the king's chamber, and as often as he woke, Irene or Curdie, whichever was watching, took the sleeping child and laid her in his arms, upon which, invariably and instantly, the dream would vanish. A great part of the day too she would be playing on or about the king's bed; and it was a delight to the heart of the princess to see her amusing herself with the crown, now sitting upon it, now rolling it hither and thither about the room like a hoop. Her grandmother entering once while she was pretending to make porridge in it, held up her hands in horror-struck amazement; but the king would not allow her to interfere, for the king was now Barbara's playmate, and his crown their plaything.

The colonel of the guard also was growing better. Curdie went often to see him. They were soon friends, for the best people understand each other the easiest, and the grim old warrior loved the miner boy as if he were at once his son and his angel. He was very anxious about his regiment. He said the officers were mostly honest men, he believed, but how they might be doing without him, or what they might resolve, in ignorance of the real state of affairs, and exposed to every misrepresentation, who could tell? Curdie proposed that he should send for the major, offering to be the messenger. The colonel agreed, and Curdie went – not without his mattock, because of the dogs.

But the officers had been told by the master of the horse that their colonel was dead, and although they were amazed he should be buried without the attendance of his regiment, they never doubted the information. The handwriting itself of their colonel was insufficient, counteracted by the fresh reports daily current, to destroy the lie. The major regarded the letter as a trap for the next officer in command, and sent his orderly to arrest the messenger. But Curdie had had the wisdom not to wait for an answer.

The king's enemies said that he had first poisoned the good colonel of the guard, and then murdered the master of the horse, and other faithful councillors; and that his oldest and most attached domestics had but escaped from the palace with their lives – not all of them, for the butler was missing. Mad or wicked, he was not only unfit to rule any longer, but worse than unfit to have in his power and under his influence the young princess, only hope of Gwyntystorm and the kingdom.

The moment the lord chancellor reached his house in the country and had got himself clothed, he began to devise how yet to destroy his master; and the very next morning set out for the neighbouring kingdom of Borsagrass to invite invasion, and offer a compact with its monarch.

CHAPTER THIRTY

Peter

AT the cottage in the mountain everything for a time went on just as before. It was indeed dull without Curdie, but as often as they looked at the emerald it was gloriously green, and with nothing to fear or regret, and everything to hope, they required little comforting. One morning, however, at last, Peter, who had been consulting the gem, rather now from habit than anxiety, as a farmer his barometer in undoubtful weather, turned suddenly to his wife, the stone in his hand, and held it up with a look of ghastly dismay.

'Why, that's never the emerald!' said Joan.

'It is,' answered Peter; 'but it were small blame to any one that took it for a bit of bottle glass!'

For, all save one spot right in the centre, of intensest and most brilliant green, it looked as if the colour had been burnt out of it.

'Run, run, Peter!' cried his wife. 'Run and tell the old princess. It may not be too late. The boy must be lying at death's door.'

Without a word Peter caught up his mattock, darted from the cottage, and was at the bottom of the hill in less time than he usually took to get halfway.

The door of the king's house stood open; he rushed in and

up the stair. But after wandering about in vain for an hour, opening door after door, and finding no way farther up, the heart of the old man had well-nigh failed him. Empty rooms, empty rooms! — desertion and desolation everywhere.

At last he did come upon the door to the tower stair. Up he darted. Arrived at the top, he found three doors, and, one after the other, knocked at them all, But there was neither voice nor hearing. Urged by his faith and his dread, slowly, hesitatingly, he opened one. It revealed a bare garret room, nothing in it but one chair and one spinning wheel. He closed it, and opened the next — to start back in terror, for he saw nothing but a great gult, a moonless night, full of stars, and, for all the stars, dark, dark!—a fathomless abyss. He opened the third door, and a rush like the tide of a living sea invaded his ears. Multitudinous wings flapped and flashed in the sun, and, like the ascending column from a volcano, white birds innumerable shot into the air, darkening the day with the shadow of their cloud, and then, with a sharp sweep, as if bent sideways by a sudden wind, flew northward, swiftly away, and vanished. The place felt like a tomb. There seemed no breath of life left in it.

Despair laid hold upon him; he rushed down thundering with heavy feet. Out upon him darted the housekeeper like an ogress-spider, and after her came her men; but Peter rushed past them, heedless and careless — for had not the princess mocked him? — and sped along the road to Gwyntystorm. What help lay in a miner's mattock, a man's arm, a father's heart, he would bear to his boy.

Joan sat up all night waiting his return, hoping and hoping. The mountain was very still, and the sky was clear; but all night long the miner sped northward, and the heart of his wife was troubled.

CHAPTER THIRTY-ONE

The Sacrifice

THINGS in the palace were in a strange condition: the king playing with a child and dreaming wise dreams, waited upon by a little princess with the heart of a queen, and a youth from the mines, who went nowhere, not even into the king's chamber, without his mattock on his shoulder and a horrible animal at his heels; in a room nearby the colonel of his guard, also in bed, without a soldier to obey him; in six other rooms, far apart, six miscreants, each watched by a beast-jailer; ministers to them all, an old woman and a page; and in the wine cellar, forty-three animals, creatures more grotesque than ever brain of man invented. None dared approach its gates, and seldom one issued from them.

All the dwellers in the city were united in enmity to the palace. It swarmed with evil spirits, they said, whereas the evil spirits were in the city, unsuspected. One consequence of their presence was that, when the rumour came that a great army was on the march against Gwyntystorm, instead of rushing to their defences, to make new gates, free portcullises and drawbridges, and bar the river, each band flew first to their treasures, burying them in their cellars and gardens, and hiding them behind stones in their chimneys; and, next to rebellion, signing an invitation to His Majesty of Borsagrass to enter at their open gates, destroy their king, and annex their country to his own.

The straits of isolation were soon found in the palace: its invalids were requiring stronger food, and what was to be done? For if the butchers sent meat to the palace, was it not likely enough to be poisoned? Curdie said to Derba he would think of some plan before morning.

But that same night, as soon as it was dark, Lina came to her master, and let him understand she wanted to go out. He unlocked a little private postern for her, left it so that she could push it open when she returned, and told the crocodile to stretch himself across it inside. Before midnight she came back with a young deer.

Early the next morning the legserpent crept out of the wine cellar, through the broken door behind, shot into the river, and soon appeared in the kitchen with a splendid sturgeon. Every night Lina went out hunting, and every morning Legserpent went out fishing, and both invalids and household had plenty to eat. As to news, the page, in plain clothes, would now and then venture out into the market place, and gather some.

One night he came back with the report that the army of the king of Borsagrass had crossed the border. Two days after, he brought the news that the enemy was now but twenty miles from Gwyntystorm.

The colonel of the guard rose, and began furbishing his armour — but gave it over to the page, and staggered across to the barracks, which were in the next street. The sentry took him for a ghost or worse, ran into the guardroom, bolted the door, and stopped his ears. The poor colonel, who was yet hardly able to stand, crawled back despairing.

For Curdie, he had already, as soon as the first rumour reached him, resolved, if no other instructions came, and the king continued unable to give orders, to call Lina and the creatures, and march to meet the enemy. If he died, he died for the right, and there was a right end of it. He had no preparations to make, except a good sleep.

He asked the king to let the housemaid take his place by His Majesty that night, and went and lay down on the floor of the corridor, no farther off than a whisper would reach from the door of the chamber. There, with an old mantle of the king's thrown over him, he was soon fast asleep.

Somewhere about the middle of the night, he woke suddenly, started to his feet, and rubbed his eyes. He could not tell what had waked him. But could he be awake, or was he not dreaming? The curtain of the king's door, a dull red ever before, was glowing a gorgeous, a radiant purple; and the crown wrought upon it in silks and gems was flashing as if it burned! What could it mean? Was the king's chamber on fire? He darted to the door and lifted the curtain. Glorious terrible sight!

A long and broad marble table, that stood at one end of the room, had been drawn into the middle of it, and thereon burned a great fire, of a sort that Curdie knew — a fire of glowing, flaming roses, red and white. In the midst of the roses lay the king, moaning, but motionless. Every rose that fell from the table to the floor, someone, whom Curdie could not plainly see for the brightness, lifted and laid burning upon the king's face, until at length his face too was covered with the live roses, and he lay all within the fire, moaning still, with now and then a shuddering sob.

And the shape that Curdie saw and could not see, wept over the king as he lay in the fire, and often she hid her face in handfuls of her shadowy hair, and from her hair the water of her weeping dropped like sunset rain in the light of the roses. At last she lifted a great armful of her hair, and shook it over the fire, and the drops fell from it in showers, and they did not hiss in the flames, but there arose instead as it were the sound of running brooks.

And the glow of the red fire died away, and the glow of the white fire grew grey, and the light was gone, and on the table all was black — except the face of the king, which shone from under the burnt roses like a diamond in the ashes of a furnace.

Then Curdie, no longer dazzled, saw and knew the old princess. The room was lighted with the splendour of her face, of her blue eyes, of her sapphire crown. Her golden hair went streaming out from her through the air till it went off in mist and light. She was large and strong as a Titaness. She stooped over the table-altar, put her mighty arms under the living sacrifice, lifted the king, as if he were but a little child, to her bosom, walked with him up the floor, and laid him in his bed. Then darkness fell.

The miner boy turned silent away, and laid himself down again in the corridor. An absolute joy filled his heart, his bosom, his head, his whole body. All was safe; all was well. With the helve of his mattock tight in his grasp, he sank into a dreamless sleep.

CHAPTER THIRTY-TWO

The King's Army

HE woke like a giant refreshed with wine.

When he went into the king's chamber, the housemaid sat where he had left her, and everything in the room was as it had been the night before, save that a heavenly odour of roses filled the air of it. He went up to the bed. The king opened his eyes, and the soul of perfect health shone out of them. Nor was Curdie amazed in his delight.

'Is it not time to rise, Curdie?' said the king.

'It is, Your Majesty. Today we must be doing,' answered Curdie.

'What must we be doing today, Curdie?'

'Fighting, sire.'

'Then fetch me my armour— that of plated steel, in the chest there. You will find the underclothing with it.'

As he spoke, he reached out his hand for his sword, which hung in the bed before him, drew it, and examined the blade.

'A little rusty!' he said, 'but the edge is there. We shall polish it ourselves today — not on the wheel. Curdie, my son, I wake from a troubled dream. A glorious torture has ended it, and I live. I know now well how things are, but you shall explain them to me as I get on my armour. No, I need no bath.

I am clean. Call the colonel of the guard.'

In complete steel the old man stepped into the chamber. He knew it not, but the old princess had passed through his room in the night.

'Why, Sir Bronzebeard!' said the king, 'you are dressed before me! You need no valet, old man, when there is battle in the wind!'

'Battle, sire!' returned the colonel. 'Where then are our soldiers?'

'Why, there and here,' answered the king, pointing to the colonel first, and then to himself. 'Where else, man? The enemy will be upon us ere sunset, if we be not upon him ere noon. What other thing was in your brave brain when you donned your armour, friend?'

'Your Majesty's orders, sire,' answered Sir Bronzebeard.

The king smiled and turned to Curdie.

'And what was in yours, Curdie, for your first word was of battle?'

'See, Your Majesty,' answered Curdie; 'I have polished my mattock. If Your Majesty had not taken the command, I would have met the enemy at the head of my beasts, and died in comfort, or done better.'

'Brave boy!' said the king. 'He who takes his life in his hand is the only soldier. You shall head your beasts today. Sir Bronzehead, will you die with me if need be?'

'Seven times, my king,' said the colonel.

'Then shall we win this battle!' said the king. 'Curdie, go and bind securely the six, that we lose not their guards. Can you find me a horse, think you, Sir Bronzebeard? Alas! they told me my white charger was dead.'

'I will go and fright the varletry with my presence, and

193

secure, I trust, a horse for Your Majesty, and one for myself.'

'And look you, brother!' said the king; 'bring one for my miner boy too, and a sober old charger for the princess, for she too must go to the battle, and conquer with us.'

'Pardon me, sire,' said Curdie; 'a miner can fight best on foot. I might smite my horse dead under me with a missed blow. And besides that, I must be near to my beasts.'

'As you will,' said the king. 'Three horses then, Sir Bronzebeard.'

The colonel departed, doubting sorely in his heart how to accoutre and lead from the barrack stables three horses, in the teeth of his revolted regiment.

In the hall he met the housemaid.

'Can you lead a horse?' he asked.

'Yes, sir.'

'Are you willing to die for the king?'

'Yes, sir.'

'Can you do as you are bid?'

'I can keep on trying, sir.'

'Come then. Were I not a man I would be a woman such as you.'

When they entered the barrack yard, the soldiers scattered like autumn leaves before a blast of winter. They went into the stable unchallenged – and lo! in a stall, before the colonel's eyes, stood the king's white charger, with the royal saddle and bridle hung high beside him!

'Traitorous thieves!' muttered the old man in his beard, and went along the stalls, looking for his own black charger. Having found him, he returned to saddle first the king's. But the maid had already the saddle upon him, and so girt that the colonel could thrust no finger tip between girth and skin. He left her to finish what she had so well begun, and went and made ready his own. He then chose for the princess a great red horse, twenty years old, which he knew to possess every equine virtue. This and his own he led to the palace, and the maid led the king's.

The king and Curdie stood in the court, the king in full armour of silvered steel, with a circlet of rubies and diamonds round his helmet. He almost leaped for joy when he saw his great white charger come in, gentle as a child to the hand of the housemaid. But when the horse saw his master in his armour, he reared and bounded in jubilation, yet did not break from the hand that held him. Then out came the princess attired and ready, with a hunting knife her father had given her by her side. They brought her mother's saddle, splendent with gems and gold, set it on the great red horse, and lifted her to it. But the saddle was so big, and the horse so tall, that the child found no comfort in them.

'Please, King Papa,' she said, 'can I not have my white pony?'

'I did not think of him, little one,' said the king. 'Where is he?'

'In the stable,' answered the maid. 'I found him half starved, the only horse within the gates, the day after the servants were driven out. He has been well fed since.'

'Go and fetch him,' said the king.

As the maid appeared with the pony, from a side door came Lina and the forty-nine, following Curdie.

'I will go with Curdie and the Uglies,' cried the princess; and as soon as she was mounted she got into the middle of the pack.

So out they set, the strangest force that ever went against an enemy. The king in silver armour sat stately on his white steed, with the stones flashing on his helmet; beside him the grim old colonel, armed in steel, rode his black charger; behind the king, a little to the right, Curdie walked afoot, his mattock shining in the sun; Lina followed at his heel; behind her came the wonderful company of Uglies; in the midst of them rode the gracious little Irene, dressed in blue, and mounted on the prettiest of white ponies; behind the colonel, a little to the left, walked the page, armed in a breastplate, headpiece, and trooper's sword he had found in the palace, all much too big for him, and carrying a huge brass trumpet which he did his best to blow; and the king smiled and seemed pleased with his music, although it was but the grunt of a brazen unrest. Alongside the beasts walked Derba carrying Barbara – their refuge the mountains, should the cause of the king be lost; as soon as they were over the river they turned aside to ascend the cliff, and there awaited the forging of the day's history. Then first Curdie saw that the housemaid, whom they had all forgotten, was following, mounted on the great red horse, and seated in the royal saddle.

Many were the eyes unfriendly of women that had stared at them from door and window as they passed through the city; and low laughter and mockery and evil words from the lips of children had rippled about their ears; but the men were all gone to welcome the enemy, the butchers the first, the king's guard the last. And now on the heels of the king's army rushed out the women and children also, to gather flowers and branches, wherewith to welcome their conquerors.

About a mile down the river, Curdie, happening to look behind him, saw the maid, whom he had supposed gone with Derba, still following on the great red horse. The same moment the king, a few paces in front of him, caught sight of the enemy's tents, pitched where, the cliffs receding, the bank of the river widened to a little plain.

CHAPTER THIRTY-THREE

The Battle

HE commanded the page to blow his trumpet; and, in the strength of the moment, the youth uttered a right warlike defiance.

But the butchers and the guard, who had gone over armed to the enemy, thinking that the king had come to make his peace also, and that it might thereafter go hard with them, rushed at once to make short work with him, and both secure and commend themselves. The butchers came on first — for the guards had slackened their saddle girths — brandishing their knives, and talking to their dogs. Curdie and the page, with Lina and her pack, bounded to meet them. Curdie struck down the foremost with his mattock. The page, finding his sword too much for him, threw it away and seized the butcher's knife, which as he rose he plunged into the foremost dog. Lina rushed raging and gnashing among them. She would not look at a dog so long as there was a butcher on his legs, and she never stopped to kill a butcher, only with one grind of her jaws crushed a leg of him. When they were all down, then indeed she flashed among the dogs.

Meantime the king and the colonel had spurred toward the advancing guard. The king clove the major through skull and collar bone, and the colonel stabbed the captain in the throat. Then a fierce combat commenced — two against many. But the butchers and their dogs quickly disposed of, up came Curdie and his beasts. The horses of the guard, struck with terror, turned in spite of the spur, and fled in confusion.

Thereupon the forces of Borsagrass, which could see little of the affair, but correctly imagined a small determined body in front of them, hastened to the attack. No sooner did their first advancing wave appear through the foam of the retreating one, than the king and the colonel and the page, Curdie and the beasts, went charging upon them. Their attack, especially the rush of the Uglies, threw the first line into great confusion, but the second came up quickly; the beasts could not be everywhere, there were thousands to one against them, and the king and his three companions were in the greatest possible danger.

A dense cloud came over the sun, and sank rapidly toward the earth. The cloud moved all together, and yet the thousands of white flakes of which it was made up moved each for itself in ceaseless and rapid motion: those flakes were the wings of pigeons. Down swooped the birds upon the invaders; right in the face of man and horse they flew with swift-beating wings, blinding eyes and confounding brain. Horses reared and plunged and wheeled. All was at once in confusion. The men made frantic efforts to seize their tormentors, but not one could they touch; and they outdoubled them in numbers. Between every wild clutch came a peck and a buffet of pinion in the face. Generally the bird would, with sharp-clapping wings, dart its whole body, with the swiftness of an arrow, against its singled mark, yet so as to glance aloft the same instant, and descend skimming; much as the thin stone, shot with horizontal cast of arm, having touched and torn the surface of the lake, ascends to skim, touch, and tear again. So mingled the feathered multitude in the grim game of war. It was a storm in which the wind was birds, and the sea men. And ever as each bird arrived at the rear of the enemy, it turned, ascended, and sped to the front to charge again.

The moment the battle began, the princess's pony took fright, and turned and fled. But the maid wheeled her horse across the road and stopped him; and they waited together the result of the battle.

And as they waited, it seemed to the princess right strange that the pigeons, every one as it came to the rear, and fetched a compass to gather force for the reattack, should make the head of her attendant on the red horse the goal around which it turned; so that about them was an unintermittent flapping and flashing of wings, and a curving, sweeping torrent of the side-poised wheeling bodies of birds. Strange also it seemed that the maid should be constantly waving her arm toward the battle. And the time of the motion of her arm so fitted with the rushes of birds, that it looked as if the birds obeyed her gesture, and she was casting living javelins by the thousand against the enemy. The moment a pigeon had rounded her head, it went off straight as bolt from bow, and with trebled velocity.

But of these strange things, others besides the princess had taken note. From a rising ground whence they watched the battle in growing dismay, the leaders of the enemy saw the maid and her motions, and, concluding her an enchantress, whose were the airy legions humiliating them, set spurs to their horses, made a circuit, outflanked the king, and came down upon her. But suddenly by her side stood a stalwart old man in the garb of a miner, who, as the general rode at her, sword in hand, heaved his swift mattock, and brought it down with such force on the forehead of his charger, that he fell to the ground like a log. His rider shot over his head and lay stunned. Had not the great red horse reared and wheeled, he would have fallen beneath that of the general.

With lifted sabre, one of his attendant officers rode at the miner. But a mass of pigeons darted in the faces of him and his horse, and the next moment he lay beside his commander. The rest of them turned and fled, pursued by the birds.

'Ah, friend Peter!' said the maid; 'thou hast come as I told thee! Welcome and thanks!'

By this time the battle was over. The rout was general. The enemy stormed back upon their own camp, with the beasts roaring in the midst of them, and the king and his army, now reinforced by one, pursuing. But presently the king drew rein.

'Call off your hounds, Curdie, and let the pigeons do the rest,' he shouted, and turned to see what had become of the princess.

In full panic fled the invaders, sweeping down their tents, stumbling over their baggage, trampling on their dead and wounded, ceaselessly pursued and buffeted by the white-winged army of heaven. Homeward they rushed the road they had come, straight for the borders, many dropping from pure fatigue, and lying where they fell. And still the pigeons were in their necks as they ran. At length to the eyes of the king and his army nothing was visible save a dust cloud below, and a bird cloud above.

Before night the bird cloud came back, flying high over Gwyntystorm. Sinking swiftly, it disappeared among the ancient roofs of the palace.

CHAPTER THIRTY-FOUR

Judgement

THE king and his army returned, bringing with them one prisoner only, the lord chancellor. Curdie had dragged him from under a fallen tent, not by the hand of a man, but by the foot of a mule.

When they entered the city, it was still as the grave. The citizens had fled home. 'We must submit,' they cried, 'or the king and his demons will destroy us.' The king rode through the streets in silence, ill-pleased with his people. But he stopped his horse in the midst of the market place, and called, in a voice loud and clear as the cry of a silver trumpet. 'Go and find your own. Bury your dead, and bring home your wounded.' Then he turned him gloomily to the palace.

Just as they reached the gates, Peter, who, as they went, had been telling his tale to Curdie, ended it with the words:

'And so there I was, in the nick of time to save the two princesses!'

'The *two* princesses, Father! The one on the great red horse was the housemaid,' said Curdie, and ran to open the gates for the king.

They found Derba returned before them, and already busy preparing them food. The king put up his charger with his own hands, rubbed him down, and fed him.

When they had washed, and eaten and drunk, he called the colonel, and told Curdie and the page to bring out the traitors and the beasts, and attend him to the market place.

By this time the people were crowding back into the city, bearing their dead and wounded. And there was lamentation in Gwyntystorm, for no one could comfort himself, and no one had any to comfort him. The nation was victorious, but the people were conquered.

The king stood in the centre of the market place, upon the steps of the ancient cross. He had laid aside his helmet and put on his crown, but he stood all armed beside, with his sword in his hand. He called the people to him, and, for all the terror of the beasts, they dared not disobey him. Those, even, who were carrying their wounded laid them down, and drew near trembling.

Then the king said to Curdie and the page:

'Set the evil men before me.'

He looked upon them for a moment in mingled anger and pity, then turned to the people and said:

'Behold your trust! Ye slaves, behold your leaders! I would have freed you, but ye would not be free. Now shall ye be ruled with a rod of iron, that ye may learn what freedom is, and love it and seek it. These wretches I will send where they shall mislead you no longer.'

He made a sign to Curdie, who immediately brought up the legserpent. To the body of the animal they bound the lord chamberlain, speechless with horror. The butler began to shriek and pray, but they bound him on the back of Clubhead. One after another, upon the largest of the creatures they bound the whole seven, each through the unveiling terror looking the villain he was. Then said the king:

'I thank you, my good beasts; and I hope to visit you ere long. Take these evil men with you, and go to your place.'

Like a whirlwind they were in the crowd, scattering it like dust. Like hounds they rushed from the city, their burdens howling and raving.

What became of them I never heard.

Then the king turned once more to the people and said, 'Go to your houses'; nor vouchsafed them another word. They crept home like chidden hounds.

The king returned to the palace. He made the colonel a duke, and the page a knight, and Peter he appointed general of all his mines. But to Curdie he said:

'You are my own boy, Curdie. My child cannot choose but love you, and when you are grown up – if you both will – you shall marry each other, and be king and queen when I am gone. Till then be the king's Curdie.'

Irene held out her arms to Curdie. He raised her in his, and she kissed him.

'And my Curdie too!' she said.

Thereafter the people called him Prince Conrad; but the king always called him either just *Curdie*, or *my miner boy*.

They sat down to supper, and Derba and the knight and the housemaid waited, and Barbara sat at the king's left hand. The housemaid poured out the wine; and as she poured for Curdie red wine that foamed in the cup, as if glad to see the light whence it had been banished so long, she looked him in the eyes. And Curdie started, and sprang from his seat, and dropped on his knees, and burst into tears. And the maid said with a smile, such as none but one could smile:

'Did I not tell you, Curdie, that it might be you would not

know me when next you saw me?'

Then she went from the room, and in a moment returned in royal purple, with a crown of diamonds and rubies, from under which her hair went flowing to the floor, all about her ruby-slippered feet. Her face was radiant with joy, the joy overshadowed by a faint mist as of unfulfilment. The king rose and kneeled on one knee before her. All kneeled in like homage. Then the king would have yielded her his royal chair. But she made them all sit down, and with her own hands placed at the table seats for Derba and the page. Then in ruby crown and royal purple she served them all.

CHAPTER THIRTY-FIVE

The End

THE king sent Curdie out into his dominions to search for men and women that had human hands. And many such he found, honest and true, and brought them to his master. So a new and upright court was formed, and strength returned to the nation.

But the exchequer was almost empty, for the evil man had squandered everything, and the king hated taxes unwillingly paid. Then came Curdie and said to the king that the city stood upon gold. And the king sent for men wise in the ways of the earth, and they built smelting furnaces, and Peter brought miners, and they mined the gold, and smelted it, and the king coined it into money, and therewith established things well in the land.

The same day on which he found his boy, Peter set out to go home. When he told the good news to Joan, his wife, she rose from her chair and said, 'Let us go.' And they left the cottage, and repaired to Gwyntystorm. And on a mountain above the city they built themselves a warm house for their old age, high in the clear air.

As Peter mined one day, at the back of the king's wine cellar, he broke into a cavern crusted with gems, and much wealth flowed therefrom, and the king used it wisely.

Queen Irene — that was the right name of the old princess — was thereafter seldom long absent from the palace. Once or twice when she was missing, Barbara, who seemed to know of her sometimes when nobody else had a notion whither she had gone, said she was with the dear old Uglies in the wood. Curdie thought that perhaps her business might be with others there as well. All the uppermost rooms in the palace were left to her use, and when any one was in need of her help, up thither he must go. But even when she was there, he did not always succeed in finding her. She, however, always knew that such a one had been looking for her.

Curdie went to find her one day. As he ascended the last stair, to meet him came the well-known scent of her roses; and when he opened the door, lo! there was the same gorgeous room in which his touch had been glorified by her fire! And there burned the fire — a huge heap of red and white roses. Before the hearth stood the princess, an old grey-haired woman, with Lina a little behind her, slowly wagging her tail, and looking like a beast of prey that can hardly so long restrain itself from springing as to be sure of its victim. The queen was casting roses, more and more roses, upon the fire. At last she turned and said, 'Now Lina!' — and Lina dashed burrowing into the fire. There went up a black smoke and a dust, and Lina was never more seen in the palace.

Irene and Curdie were married. The old king died, and they were king and queen. As long as they lived Gwyntystorm was a better city, and good people grew in it. But they had no children, and when they died the people chose a king. And the new king went mining and mining in the rock under the city, and grew more and more eager after the gold, and paid less and less heed to his people. Rapidly they sank toward their old wickedness. But still the king went on mining, and coining gold by the pailful, until the people were worse even than in the old time. And so greedy was the king after gold, that when at last the ore began to fail, he caused the miners to reduce the pillars which Peter and they that followed him had left standing to bear the city. And from the girth of an oak of a thousand years, they chipped them down to that of a fir tree of fifty.

One day at noon, when life was at its highest, the whole city fell with a roaring crash. The cries of men and the shrieks of woman went up with its dust, and then there was a great silence.

Where the mighty rock once towered, crowded with homes and crowned with a palace, now rushes and raves a stone-obstructed rapid of the river. All around spreads a wilderness of wild deer, and the very name of Gwyntystorm has ceased from the lips of men.